West to a Land of Plenty

The Diary of Teresa Angelino Viscardi

BY JIM MURPHY

Scholastic Inc. New York

Jersey City, New Jersey

1883

EVERYONE IS WELCOME

TO A FREE SERIES OF LECTURES ON THE BENEFITS
AND REWARDS AVAILABLE IN THE WESTERN
TERRITORY OF IDAHO, WHERE LAND IS CHEAP AND
THE SOIL IS OF THE RICHEST KIND. HEAR MR.
WILSON ANDERSON, VICE-CHAIRMAN OF THE
ASSOCIATION FOR THE DEVELOPMENT OF THE
TOWN OF OPPORTUNITY, DESCRIBE THIS LAND OF
PLENTY, FREEDOM, AND ECONOMIC POTENTIAL,
WITH NO OBLIGATION TO YOU AT ALL!
REFRESHMENTS WILL BE SERVED. ALL ARE INVITED,
INCLUDING THE IRISH AND THOSE OF THE
LATIN, SLAV, SEMITIC, AND MONGOLIAN RACES.
JANUARY 14 AT 7 P.M. AT 43 SPRING STREET.

I hate this train and its tiny wood seats and the
cacarocielu crawling everywhere! And the rain. I HATE
IT!! I Hate Poppa. And Momma — for letting him do
this to us! And Uncle Eugenio — I hate him for seeing
the advertisement and for making Poppa leave our
street. And my aunt. All she thinks about is money. And
supper. And Nanna — I hate her most of al[1]

Dear Sister: A writer is only as good as her pencil, and a pencil is only as good as its point. Have I made my point? And why did you paste in the advertisement if you hate the move so much?
Your Sister, Antoinetta

Little sisters should never be seen or heard. And they should n't snoop where they are n't invited. I hate snoops — so stay away from my diary. Your Angry Sister, Teresa Angelino Viscardi. I MEAN IT!! End. And I do not have to explain why I do anything in MY diary, but if you have to know, I put the advertisement in so I will never, ever forget how I came to be here and who is responsible!

Netta is so annoying. I showed her what I wrote about her and she did n't *didn't* get upset. She just pointed to the mistakes and said, "What would Mrs. Curran say?" I hate Little Know-It-All Sisters! And Mrs. Curran would be happy that I made a start on my diary — mistakes and all. Today is Wednesday, April 4, 1883. It is after 4 o'clock, but Uncle Eugenio's pocket watch is not very good, so it might be later. End.

April 5 — I think

Does anyone know how to run this train? First, we sat in our stuffy, uncomfortable car for a long time while they added more baggage cars. Very slowly, if you ask me. Then the conductor ordered us out of the car without saying why. We had to wait on the platform in the rain and wind. Mrs. Curran said I should write down what people say, but I do n't *don't* think she would like the language I heard to describe the railroad men — tho the many accents were colorful.

Momma held an umbrella over Baby Tomas and Ernesto and herself. Ernesto didn't even help — just sat on his valise like a little king, looking at his book the whole time. He thinks he's so important because he's the oldest boy. Poppa held the other umbrella over Nanna. I had to stand with Cousin Rosaria, who didn't like sharing her umbrella, so I am more wet than dry. Baby Tomas cried and fussed, and I don't blame him at all. I felt the very same. Aunt Marta could have helped Momma with Tomas, but she didn't. Instead, she made Uncle Eugenio hold his umbrella over her while she ate bread and onion. And complained.

Then Mr. Conductor told us to go back into our car and even barked at me to hurry up. He didn't apologize for making us stand in the cold or tell us what happened. Mr. Kozwitski — who is a very big man, but as nervous as a momma bird with a full nest — tried to get an answer from him, but Mr. Conductor just turned and walked away.

The train left Jersey City after dark and went a little way before it stopped, went another little way, and stopped again. Again and again, stop-go, stop-go. I would have tried to describe the scenery — as Mrs. Curran said I should — but the mist on the windows makes it hard to see much besides black shapes. Most people in our car went to sleep long ago — which is why I think it is past midnight. Tomas is crying again, and Momma doesn't seem to be able to comfort him. I miss my bed on Wooster Street. Even sharing it with Netta — who wiggles and pulls at the quilt in her sleep — was better than this seat. We are going again. At last! End.

April 5 still

Didn't sleep much, thanks to Netta and the train's movement. One of the Irish-men — they are 5 brothers and Poppa calls them the "Irish Brigade" — sang a sad song about Bunclody or some such place. Part of it stuck in my head —

So adieu, my dear father, adieu, my dear mother,
Farewell to my sister, farewell to my brother,
I am bound for America, my fortune to try,
When I think on Bunclody, I'm ready to die.

I would have put more down, but a German-man shouted, "Stop that noise, will you? People are trying to sleep." Then Tomas started fussing, tho Momma got him quiet before the German-man said anything — but not before Aunt Marta shook her head and clucked something about a noisy train. Why does she always have to criticize Momma? Closed my eyes but my head filled with pictures of Francesca and Nicola and Mrs. Curran and others — I wonder if they are picturing me? I hope so. I am having a hard time keeping awake. Will end for now.

Still April 5!

This has been the longest day in all of my 14 years — other than when we left Wooster Street. The only good thing is that when I woke, Netta asked where my diary was and I wouldn't tell her. I will not even tell you, dear diary, where I keep you since snoopy Know-It-All Little Sisters have BIG eyes too. But I have a very safe hiding place for you, you can be assured.

The train has stopped — again — and we are sitting on a side track. Why? Who knows! The car we are in is nothing but a big shoe box with 30 wood seats on each side of the center aisle, a stove for heating and cooking at the front end, and a Convenience back here. I will not describe the Convenience or what it smells like, tho I am glad it is dark in there. The dark doesn't scare me. It is what I might see in there that scares me.

Our car is jammed with people — 2 to a seat with little ones like Tomas on laps — all of us going to Opportunity. If the train would ever move, that is. We have not even reached Philadelphia and we have been on this train over 24 hours. Mr. Conductor has not presented himself today and there is much grumbling. I will write Francesca a letter and post it at our next stop. End.

Dear Sister: If you post Francesca's letter at our next stop you will probably have to ask a friendly crow to deliver it. A hint: To keep a secret hiding place secret you should not keep looking at it when you think I am not looking at you. You can be assured of that. Your Sister still, Antoinetta.

I meant our next *REAL* stop and not a stop on a side track and Netta knew it. She just wants to show me up whenever she can. And when I told her to leave my diary alone, she smiled that annoying smile she puts on when she wants to make me angry. SHE MAKES ME *SO* ANGRY! Then Momma said I shouldn't raise my voice and should act like a proper young lady and that Netta was too young to know about diaries. She is 8 — which is old enough, if you ask me. Nanna scolded me too. She shook her finger at me and said in Italian that I should be ashamed of myself and that it was a sin. . . . But I stopped listening to her since it wasn't fair. Netta was the one who should be scolded!

Dear Francesca,

    This is the very first letter I have ever written to you. Mrs. Curran read HILL'S MANUAL to me about Letters of Friendship and it told me what I should say in my letters, but I have forgotten it all except for "go into all the little particulars, just as you would talk." I don't think I have enough paper to do that, and I don't think you want to hear them all because they aren't very happy particulars and I know how much you like happy things.

    We left Wooster Street before the sun came up, but Momma wouldn't let me wake you to say another good-bye. All 5 families from our street hired wagons for the trip to the ferry slip, people and things piled high. We went in Mr. Glenney's ice-wagon, bumping up and down the cobblestone streets *all the way.* Mr. Glenney was very nice and did not even complain when he lifted Momma's piano onto the wagon. The ferry took us across to Jersey City, rolling from side to side *all the way.* The train — when it goes — bumps up and down *and* side to side *all the time* and has a most unusual effect on the stomach. Momma has not said much to anyone since we left — except to tell me to smooth my dress or comb my hair or not talk loud. She still isn't happy about leaving New York and her family and friends — and neither am I! — but there isn't anything we can do now. Poppa does what Uncle Eugenio or Nanna says and is not as fun as he was at home. Baby Tomas cries a lot, Ernesto feels sick from the movement of the boat and train, and Netta is Netta. The cooking smells are always changing in the car because there are so many different kinds of people going to Opportunity. Nanna does not like the smells, but they make my mouth water so I think I do. I wish I was there right now to tell you all the little particulars and more. Remember to write to me in care of General Delivery and I will check every time we stop. I miss you already.

Love, Your Forever Best Friend, Teresa

P.S. Please tell Mrs. Curran that I am practicing my penmanship by writing my letters to you in the diary she gave me. I am really copying them so I know what I've said to you, and don't really copy them down very neatly, but promise you won't tell Mrs. Curran that.

Friday, April 6

I didn't write End at the end of my last entry, I was so angry at Netta and Nanna and Momma. That is all right since I have more to say about Thursday.

Yesterday after being put on another side track Poppa, Uncle Eugenio, and the men from our street began talking about finding Mr. Conductor to complain. They talked in Italian, but the other men in the car must have understood enough because soon they were all up near the stove talking — some in American, some in Italian or Polish or German. The talk got loud and angry, and Mr. Kozwitski kept telling everyone to be calm and that the train would eventually move. But Uncle Eugenio, one from the Irish Brigade — I think his name is Liam — the German-man, whose name is Mr. Hesse, and another tall man with a long nose and a stern look decided to go outside in the rain to find Mr. Conductor. Mr. Kozwitski went too, all the time asking them not to make trouble. Poppa and the other men trailed behind Mr. Kozwitski with Ernesto and the rest of the boys behind them. When I got up Momma told me to sit down because this was the men's business, and Nanna shook her finger at me and said, "You should be a good girl like Rosaria here," and Rosaria — who was still sitting with her hands folded — had to smile and say, "Thank you, Nanna," like a good girl would. Next we heard shouting — Uncle Eugenio, Liam, Mr. Hesse, and Stern Look for our side and Mr. Conductor and another railroad man covered with coal dust for theirs. Poor Mr. Kozwitski stood between the 2 sides looking upset and biting his lower lip and trying to keep everyone calm, but no one was listening to him. Mr. Conductor pointed to our car and said, "Get back in there or else!" Momma and Nanna looked worried and Nanna made the sign of the cross and began saying prayers to the Little Madonna of Trappeto. I think she was afraid we would be put off the train right there in that wild part of New Jersey. But our men did not go back inside. They stayed and told Mr. Conductor that they paid good money for a train ride so the train should be going, not sitting, and Mr. Conductor screamed, "You dirty for-ners better watch out!" and Stern Face leaned down — he is *very* tall — and said loudly, "We are American citizens as good as you!" I thought Mr. Conductor would explode, his face got so red, but then he saw that men from the other cars — who are not going to Opportunity, but are regular paying passengers — and some of the bolder women had joined our group and were saying the same things.

Mr. Conductor and Coal Dust tried to back away, but they were surrounded and couldn't go anyplace. That was when the steam whistle blew and the train started moving. Everyone — men, women, boys, Mr. Conductor, and Coal Dust — had to run and jump to get back in their cars. They were lucky the engineer let the train creep along slowly til everyone was inside. Poppa came back all wet, but smiling, and said to Momma, "There, maybe now we will get somewhere." Momma still looked worried, and Nanna shook her finger at Poppa and said in Italian, "A cock who crows too loud in the morning will be in the pot at night." Ernesto was so pleased with himself that I couldn't look at him. All he and the other boys did was stand behind the men and make silly faces. But at least the train started to move and still is. End.

9 o'clock the same night: We are in Philadelphia! — 95 miles and 51!!! hours from Jersey City. The lights are almost as bright as on Wooster Street but not as friendly. Our car was separated from the rest, and the train went off with Mr. Conductor shaking his fist and spitting at our car, but we just laughed because he slipped on the wet steps and his hat fell off and went under the metal wheels. Then our car and another with more people headed for Opportunity were added to a different train going to Chicago. You can imagine how long that took. Another leader from the group is with us now and Mr. Kozwitski looks relieved. Still raining. I will find out — if Momma lets me get up — what the new leader is like and let you know. End for now.

10 o'clock: His name is Mr. Wilson Anderson — the one who spoke last January and convinced Uncle Eugenio that we should leave New York! That seems so long ago, but I can still remember how Uncle Eugenio and Poppa came into our apartment after the second lecture. I could tell that something bad was about to happen because Poppa wouldn't look at Momma or anyone. It was Uncle Eugenio who did the talking. "The land — 20,000 acres, can you imagine?! — is all owned by this Mr. Keil. And he is not just rich. No, he is also a very generous man. He is willing to sell us plots for $200. Think of it. 160 acres! Bigger than the block this apartment is built on. You will be able to build a house of your own, not just these small rooms and rent due every first of the month or you're out on the street. He is also going to put up a school, a meetinghouse, and fix the roads with his own money." Momma said that was all very nice, but she wanted to know where we would get $200 since we barely had money for milk and coal and rent. "Don't worry," said Uncle Eugenio, "I have a little to give, and Nanna will give you the rest." Momma turned and looked first at Nanna, who said, yes, that was true. Then Momma glared at Poppa. Even I could tell that it had all been decided between Uncle Eugenio and Nanna before that night and that Poppa had gone along with them and not said anything to Momma. "I don't know," Momma whispered, shaking her head. "We'll see." What is there to see? Uncle Eugenio wanted to know, but then Poppa said he would talk to Momma. Momma does not get loud when she is angry like Aunt Marta, but Momma can be quiet in a very loud way, and I think Poppa wanted to explain things in private now that the news was out in the open.

Later, when they thought I was asleep, I heard Momma and Poppa talking. "Things are not going good at the store, Rose," Poppa said. "Eugenio says he is losing money, that people are going to that new store, where the owners are from the north, near Naples. There aren't enough around here from our village, our region." Momma said something, but she speaks so softly I couldn't hear. Then Poppa said, "But there may not be a store soon, don't you see? Eugenio says if things don't change he will have to close. And if that happens what will I do, what will *we* do? Work for people who are not from Trappeto, who will look down on me and show no respect?" There was more talk that night. Much more. But what I remember most is the way Poppa said that in Idaho he could do what he loved to do — work in his fields and his orchards. Well, he might love farming, but I don't think I will.

Momma hadn't completely given in, but then Nanna started in the next day. The air in the city is bad, she complained, we are surrounded by strangers from other villages and other countries, 9 in 1 apartment is too many, the noise from the street and too-close neighbors hurts her ears. Day after day, Nanna went on like this. Momma might say, "Oh, the noise is not so loud" or, "We are all the same in this neighborhood — poor," but it didn't change anyone else's mind. Finally, about a week later at breakfast, she announced, "Poppa says we will be leaving here in early April."

That was all Momma said before going back to the stove. She did not look happy about it, but she had agreed with the rest of the family about going. I wanted to know why she gave in, why she didn't keep on saying no, no, no, no. But Momma waved me away and said there was no need to talk about it anymore, and even I knew it was no use. Writing all this makes me feel very far from Wooster Street. End.

Saturday, April 7

Mr. Anderson came to our car to talk to us right after breakfast. I thought I would dislike him immediately, but did not. He is tall and distinguished-looking and seemed not to notice the smell of garlic and sausage and boiled potatoes and cabbage and onions. His son — who is also tall — was with him.

Mr. Anderson introduced himself and then said, "Mr. Keil has asked me to welcome you to our family and to say he is eagerly awaiting your arrival at Watertown. Each 1 of you is a pioneer in the true spirit of this country and as brave as any patriot who has fought for its liberty and settlement." He also told us that the "hardships of the journey will soon give way to the pleasures and pride of new homes and new lives, where we all work together for the community and our individual prosperity." I don't know about this as I was perfectly happy with my old home and old life, but Mr. Anderson has a nice voice and the Idaho Territory didn't seem so impossibly far away today. Time will tell. He showed us a plan for the town of Opportunity and I will draw it here:

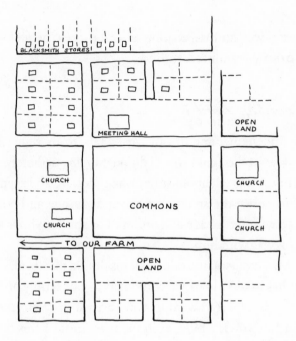

That is not a good likeness — and Netta had to say so, of course! — but it is close. The Commons is very big and everything seems open and airy. Nanna said it looked like the *chiazza* in Trappeto, only theirs had only 1 church and there was a winehouse directly across from it.

The train left Philadelphia after lunch and is still moving. We stopped in Harrisberg at 4, crossed the Suscwehana River on a big, metal bridge, and will be in Altoona later today. Over 200 miles in 10 hours! Are the tracks in Pennsylvania faster than the tracks in New Jersey? Can see mountains through rain clouds so I will go to the back platform for a better view. Mr. Anderson's son's name is John Wilson Anderson and he is 14 — the same as me. End.

Dear Sister: I am not trying to show you up, so I will not write down the best way to spell Susquehanna or Harrisburg or any other words unless you ask me. As for the map of Opportunity, it was you who asked me what I thought of it so I told you. The Commons was not a perfect rectangle but had cut-off corners, and a lane sliced it in 2 with a circle in the center. My recollection of it is this:

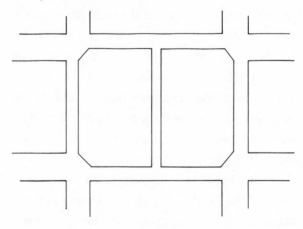

In my opinion, you were distracted by the tall Mr. Wilson Anderson or his son, the also tall Mr. John Wilson Anderson. But I could be mistaken.
Your Sister, Antoinetta

April 7 still

Mrs. Curran said I have Latin blood and am hot-tempered and should not respond to every challenge, and this is exactly what I will do with Netta from now on — other than to say I was not distracted! We are coming to Altoona. I am going to copy down my second letter to Francesca to take my mind off annoying little sisters. End.

Dear Francesca,

I miss you so much that I have to write again. Since my first letter the train has begun to move. Poppa says it can go faster and that we still make too many stops. Yesterday we were on a side track when a Pullman Express went by and I could hear an organ playing and people singing. I pictured us singing a merry tune while sitting in our own comfortable seats. Imagine that! Even without organ music, I have been thinking about you and everyone on our street and wishing I was home again. Last night I heard Momma crying, and Poppa whispered, "This is for the better, Rose, and you know it." She did not stop crying, so Poppa added, "This was our only chance to lift ourselves up, the only way I could see. Would you want the children to always live as we did back there?" Momma shook her head no, but I wanted to scream — "Back there is where Francesca lives, where my other friends live, where . . ." But I didn't say anything. Poppa seemed as sad as Momma just then and I didn't think screaming would help either of them. Instead, I prayed for a miracle that will get the engineer lost so he ends up in Jersey City by mistake. If that ever happened maybe Poppa would give up on going to the Idaho Territory. I don't think he would change his mind otherwise — not with Uncle Eugenio and Nanna here to say the opposite. We are coming to Altoona, so I will stop writing and see if there is a post office. Please tell Mrs. Curran I will write her a long letter soon.

Love, Your Friend, Teresa

Sunday, April 8

What a day! It started with Momma being upset because the train was not going to stop to let us hear mass. Many in the car were also upset that they couldn't go to their churches, but Uncle Eugenio said a train is a business and could not stop for such things. Someone sang a hymn that began, "Sweet hour of prayer! Sweet hour of prayer! Thy wings shall my petition bear . . ." Momma said it was the wrong religion and told us not to listen, and that we should say an hour of our own prayers to ourselves. I did this as best as I could, but the hymns were so pretty that sometimes I mixed up the words to the "Our Father."

Because we are behind schedule, the engineer has cut our stopping time in half. When we got to Altoona Saturday night, we had just 10 minutes to find and eat supper and return to our cars. I skipped supper and went to mail my letter, but the window was closed. A station porter said he'd mail my letter if I left my stamp pennies with him. Nanna would say I was foolish and recite 1 of her sayings, but he had a kindly way and I trusted him. He also gave me a copy of the Shaker Almanac and told me it had many wonderful pictures in it. "You might learn a thing or 2, miss," he said. "When you are finished with it, pass it on to another soul in need." Maybe he thought I could not speak American very well because he spoke every word so slow and clear. I said thank you, and that I was sure I would enjoy learning new things from it — and I said this very fast, which surprised the man and made him laugh — and then I hid the almanac in my dress pocket. Momma does not trust the Irish and they are Catholic like us. I don't think she would think much of anything Shaker.

I did not try to look at the almanac right away, even tho I wanted to very much. I waited til dark and went to the car platform to look at my new treasure in private. There was hardly a bit of light to see, but I could tell the porter was right. It has many pictures of old Shaker women making their Shaker Extract of Roots and it talks of the diseases it can cure — which seems to be all of them according to the almanac.

We started chugging around a big turn just then. I don't know why I did it but I looked up and down the length of the train and saw that 1 car behind us another person had also put their head out from the platform. It was a boy and when he saw me looking at him he pulled his head back in fast. I could be wrong, but I think it was John Wilson Anderson. End.

Monday, April 9

A very bad thing has happened! Netta knows about the Shaker Almanac and said she would tell Momma unless I let her read my diary *and* let her write in it. I will not say what should happen to little sisters like Netta. It would be a sin and anyway she would probably tell Momma and get me in more trouble. I think I will never write in this diary again! Ever!!! The End.

Monday, April 9, 1883

This is the first time I am writing in Teresa's diary and do not have to hide from her. She is sitting with Momma and is sulking. I hope she feels better soon. Aria said her diary has a name. She said every proper diary has to have a name. I will call you Aria after my friend. I will talk to Aria the diary directly and maybe I will not miss Aria my friend so much. It has stopped raining. I am going to eat an apple now and then count cows.

Yours, Antoinetta

Monday, April 9, 1883, leaving Pittsburgh

Dear Aria,

We had to change cars in Pittsburgh. Momma, Nanna, and Teresa did most of the packing. I took care of Tomas. There are now three cars going to Opportunity, plus Mr. Wilson Anderson's private car. Two cars hold families. The other has single men. The Irish brothers had to leave our car and were replaced by a family of seven. Momma thinks they are from Bohemia, though they all speak American so it is hard to tell. Mr. Anderson had his car placed between the single men and the families and Nanna said, "A good fence keeps the fox from the chickens." I do not see why it is necessary. The single men all seemed very friendly and nice. A car of China-men was put in the front, so we are not as close to the engine smoke and can open our windows more. The China-men are not going to Opportunity. They are going to work on the railroad in the north. Our new car is the same as the old car, except it smells of lye soap and carbolic acid. Teresa is still annoyed, but she has not scowled at me today. Maybe it would cheer her up if I let her use my pocket dictionary. If Teresa used it there would be no misspelled words for me to worry over. Momma is at the stove in the front of the car making us soup with spinach, onions, peas, and a bone she got in Pittsburgh. Poppa ate the last of the crusty bread we brought from home and said he will never eat the soft kind they sell at the train stations. I like the soft bread. It does not hurt my mouth.

Yours, Antoinetta

Tuesday, April 10, 1883, in Ohio

Dear Aria,

I asked Teresa if she wanted to write in her diary and she said she had nothing to say to it or me. I do not believe this be-cause she has been on the car platform many times today. Once I could see only the bottom of her dress and her shoes on the ladder. She must have seen something interesting out there. The land is very flat and gray, so she cannot be looking at it all this time. I will find out. It is raining again.

Yours, Antoinetta

Wednesday, April 11, 1883, in Ohio

Dear Aria,

I said five prayers this morning. Two to the Little Madonna of Trappeto, one to the Sweet Baby Jesus, one to His Holy Father in Heaven, and one to Saint Anselm of the Five Wounds. I want them to get Teresa to write in her diary again. It is no fun reading what I already know.

Yours, Antoinetta

Thursday, April 12, 1883, in Illinois

Dear Aria,

It is very warm in the car and the smoke from the cigars and cigarettes stinks. My stomach does not feel good either. Teresa has gone to the back platform again, but I do not even feel like watching her today. Do you know any news? Well, I don't.

Yours, Antoinetta

April 12

Netta has a sour stomach, and so do Poppa and Ernesto. And Aunt Marta and Cousin Rosaria. When Rosaria went to use the Convenience she stopped next to me and said, "What are you laughing at?" but I wasn't laughing or smiling or even thinking of laughing or smiling. I was about to tell her this, but she grabbed her stomach and ran for the Convenience before I could. It seems that everyone in our car is sick, and Momma thinks it is caused by the bad air and the bouncing train. Aunt Marta thinks it is the salami we brought from New York, so she threw theirs out the window. The Shaker Almanac doesn't say where a sour stomach comes from, but it does tell why everyone is marching back here to the Convenience. It says: "The food remains in the stomach until it becomes corrupted, which poisons the blood, and produces the most painful and distressing feelings. The stomach loses its tone, becomes inflamed and filled with slime and mucus." I showed this to Netta, but it did not seem to give her much comfort. I wrote out a poem from the almanac and gave it to Netta to cheer her up. It goes:

Pass the butter gently, Mabel,
  Shove it lightly through the air;
In the corner of the dish, love,
  You will find a nut brown hair.
What fond mem'ries it awakens
  Of the days ere we were wed,
When upon my fine coat collar
  Oft was laid your little head;

Lovingly I stroked those tresses,
In the happy days gone by;
Now I strike them every meal time
In the butter or the pie!

Netta looked at the poem, groaned, and curled up on the seat. If I could get a 25-cent bottle of Shaker Extract of Roots I know it would make everyone feel better.

I helped Momma with Tomas and listened to Nanna tell me how good girls in Sicily behave. According to Nanna a good girl stays indoors all the time and only talks to boys from a second-story window. A good girl never, *ever* goes for a walk with a boy unless there is a chaperone to watch them. And a good girl never talks loudly or argues. I think it must be very boring being a good girl.

Next, I went to the back platform. It is not raining today and I could see way off in the distance. I watched a farmhouse and its people and animals for a long time as they came closer and closer and got bigger and bigger, until we were even with them. Then they got smaller and smaller as they moved farther away until they disappeared from sight. Everything moved very slowly and peacefully. But if I looked down close to the train, the ground and rails and weeds and rocks rushed by in a gray-brown blur and I couldn't sort any of it out. That's what this journey is like — a gray-brown blur that makes my head spin. I even have a hard time seeing the faces of my friends from home and remembering what a day was like back there. Slow for 1 thing and more steady than a jolty train ride. I wonder if all of my old thoughts will fade away — like the farmhouse and people and animals? That is why I have decided to write in my diary again. To help me remember better. End.

1 thing more: When the train went around a sharp bend, I saw John Wilson Anderson on his platform looking at the farmhouse. I don't know why I did it, but I waved and guess what? He waved back! Nanna is always saying I should have more friends, but I am not sure she would approve of this boldness. But I don't care! I am not a good girl in Sicily! End again.

Thursday, April 12, 1883, near Chicago

Dear Aria,

Netta was unhappy when she saw that I did not write Dear Aria or the day or year and such. I think it is a waste of space to say these things again and again. Who made up such silly rules about writing in a diary anyway? I said this to Netta and her stomach began to hurt a lot, so I will do it — at least until she is better.

I will not be able to write much else because the lights of Chicago are in sight. Poppa said the journey to Chicago should have taken 2 or 3 days. It is now day 8. He also promised that 1 day I would be happy in our new home. I am going to the back platform 1 more time and hope that the train goes around another sharp bend. End.

Sincerely, Teresa Angelino Viscardi

Dear Mrs. Curran,

I had planned to write you a long and full letter when we arrived in Chicago, tho I do not know how much time I will have. When we arrived we were told our next train left from another station — 10 blocks away! — and we spent most of our time finding a wagon and moving our belongings. The man was not happy when he saw Momma's piano and charged an extra $1 to take it.

The station is crowded and I think everyone is angry with the railroad. We were told the heavy rains washed out many crossings and telegraph lines and that all trains to and from

Chicago are being rerouted, even the First Class Express trains. A man in a silk top hat shook his cane at a porter and demanded that he get his train moving "this very instant." The porter tipped his cap in a very dignified manner and said, "Yes, sir, and I will personally pull it across the river as well," and then walked off shaking his head.

I am writing in the diary you gave me, tho not every day as I had hoped. I will try to do better. I have worked on my -ible and -able words and have filled a page with each. Netta said what I was doing was very "admirable," tho my penmanship was sometimes not very "legible." She is ill, so I did not say a word in reply. Netta has let me use her pocket dictionary and I have looked up several words in this letter to be sure their spelling is correct.

I will close now and send this to you from here. Poppa says it will be "another lifetime" before the railroad men have the train made up, which I think means that it will be another hour or so before we can board. And then it will be on to Watertown, in the Dakota Territory!

Your Former Student, Teresa Viscardi

Friday, April 13, 1883
Somewhere between Chicago and Joliet

Dear Aria,

The train is racing along — Uncle Eugenio said we would get to Joliet in less than an hour and it is over 40 miles from Chicago! Except for Nanna — who is upset because we did not have time enough in Chicago to find a shop that sells crusty bread or salamis or the herbs she needs for her cooking — everyone seems happier now that the train is going fast. Even the new conductor we have is cheerful. He came into our car and announced, "Welcome to the Burlington, Cedar Rapids & Northern Railroad" and told us that to make up time, Joliet would be the only stop in all of Illinois, except for Rock Island, the last stop in the state. Then he tipped his cap and told us to have a nice day. Momma was so surprised, she said, "Imagine that!" in American.

Sincerely, Teresa Angelino Viscardi

Still Friday, April 13, 1883, passing Minooka

Dear Aria,

Saw a strange sight today. Just outside of Minooka there was a large team of horses — 40 or more — *and* men, maybe 50 of them — all pulling a 2-story house down the road. The house was up on a platform with long wood runners and was sliding along the dirt road. A boy sitting on the rooftop waved a red flag at the train. Wouldn't it be nice if we could take our building on Wooster Street to the Idaho Territory with all our friends inside! End.

Sincerely, Teresa Viscardi

Friday, April 13, 1883, in Illinois

Dear Aria,

I am feeling much better, thank you, and so are Poppa, Ernesto, and Aunt Marta. A few people are still sick, so the door to the Convenience is always opening and closing. Bang, bang, bang. Nanna scolded Teresa for putting her shoes on the back of the seat, and when Teresa said, "But Nanna . . ." Nanna snapped, "Stop with this American way of saying things. It is Nonna. Call me Nonna." "Here in America, it is Nanna," Teresa said fiercely and then stared out the window. Teresa looked angry so I read from the Shaker Almanac where it says, "a despondent person ought never to eat blue fish." Teresa tried to stay angry, but could not. First she giggled, then she laughed out loud. Nanna said something about girls laughing too loud, and Teresa laughed even louder. The Shaker Almanac is wonderful medicine, I think.

Yours in sickness and in health, Antoinetta

Friday, April 13, 1883, in Illinois

Dear Aria,

I was just wondering if I would ever grow up into being an Antoinetta or if I would be a Netta all of my life. Teresa said stop thinking such silly things, but I do not think it is so silly.

Yours, Antoinetta

Friday, April 13, 1883, over the Mississippi River

Dear Aria,

We are on a great stone-and-steel bridge that crosses the Mississippi River. The train is creeping along and the bridge is making terrible noises, but not so loud that I couldn't hear Mr. Hesse tell Liam of the Irish Brigade that a bridge just like this 1 fell down in Scotland with a train on it. Momma says it is not lady-like to listen to other people talking, but I noticed that right after Mr. Hesse said this, Momma crossed herself. I did too. I learned to spell Mississippi from a sign in Rock Island for MISSISSIPPI TASTING WHISKY: NOT A HEADACHE IN A GALLON. End.

Sincerely, Teresa Viscardi

Same, same, same, but in Iowa somewhere

Dear Aria,

Mr. Wilson Anderson comes through our car every day to answer questions, about Opportunity. There are not many questions, really — just pleasant nods, hellos, and such. Even Mr. Hesse — who has hundreds of things to complain about the rest of the time — is very quiet around Mr. Anderson. Everyone is impressed by him, and when he talks about Mr. Keil's vision of the town and the forests and streams and good growing soil in Idaho, it all seems real and much different from the prairie we are crossing now. Poppa even began telling us what sort of crops he might plant. John Wilson Anderson has begun to appear with his father, and Netta said she caught him looking at me once — whatever that means. Netta says she wants to say something important to you so I will End here.
Sincerely, TAV

Friday, April 13, 1883, in Iowa

Dear Aria,

I have decided that I like being Netta and do not want to change into an Antoinetta. I will continue to sign my name Antoinetta. I think it looks and sounds elegant and will be useful if I ever meet a king.
Yours, Antoinetta

Dear Francesca,

The train is still moving. Unfortunately, it is moving west, and New York and you are farther and farther away. There has been much talk in the train about Indians and buffalo and wolves since we left Chicago, but all we have seen here in Iowa are great square fields of corn stubble, tiny towns, sturdy barns, and unpainted farmhouses. And lots of cattle, horses, and chickens. And a few pigs. Poppa said the only thing flatter than Iowa is the top of a straw hat, but I don't think that is true. The flat part, I mean. There are lots of little hills and gullies — wave after wave of them, tho there aren't many trees in sight. Everyone in the car is tired and quiet today. Even the boys have stopped play shooting each other. The sun is out at last and makes it very warm in here. Today I saw a farmer and his dog on a red and green wagon. The dog barked at the train and wagged his tail, but the farmer didn't look up or tip his hat hello. He stayed hunched over, flicking the reins to keep his horses moving. I hope the people in the Idaho Territory are as friendly as the dogs in Iowa. I miss you and everyone there and think of you and home every day. Every minute of every day. Every second of every minute of every day.

Love from your friend in almost flat Iowa,

Teresa

Monday, April 16, in Estherville

Dear Aria,

I have not written in a while. The reason — I have not had anything to say. Uncle Eugenio told me we had crossed about 300 miles of Iowa but it felt like 1,000 to me. I liked looking at the land and farms for the first 100 miles, but after that I had to agree with Poppa. Iowa is FLAT.

I listened to Momma reading to Poppa from the *Iowa City Press* that Ernesto found at the last station. I was tired, and Momma's whispering voice did not help keep me awake — she does not want others to know Poppa can't read. She was reading about the murder trial of a man named Alfred Packer, but I can't recall any details, other than that he was called "the ghoul of the San Juans." I must have fallen asleep, because that is all I remember of Saturday. Sunday was the same, except that Ernesto and Netta had a fight and Nanna scolded her and Momma scolded *him*! I almost said "imagine that" out loud, but Poppa was looking at me and shaking his head so I managed to hold my tongue. But only just barely.

The train got to Estherville in the middle of the night. All I remember is Momma whispering to Ernesto not to worry about the grunting, snorting sounds. Sometimes I wish that she would whisper to me like that. When I woke up I saw what was making those strange noises. We were on a track next to a pen of long-horned cattle and they did not seem happy to be in Estherville either. Netta said something about the noise to the conductor and he told her they never stop day or night. Then he said, "Except for when the meteorite hit four years back. *Boom-boom-boom.* Three mighty explosions it made just before it hit the Sever Lee Farm. So loud, even the cattle got quiet — dead quiet — for the longest while, maybe even a minute." Netta was not sure the story was true, and Poppa said be careful since people in places where the land is big sometimes make up big stories to match. I believe the conductor because he has been very nice to us all the way from Chicago. I said this to Poppa, and Nanna — who seems to hear *everything even when said in American* — said, "Even the wolf can smile when he wants to."

I am writing this on the platform where we are waiting for a new engine that will take us to Watertown in the Dakota Territory. Mr. Wilson Anderson and John

Wilson Anderson are going from family to family and are almost here. So I will stop writing to say hello.

I am so angry with Nanna and everyone else!!! Except John Wilson, that is. John Wilson didn't do anything except say hello. When he came to my family I stopped writing and waited my turn. He said hello to Nanna, then Momma and Poppa — and even bowed a little — then Ernesto, and Netta, and even Baby Tomas. I thought I would say something clever to him about standing on car platforms, but when he came to me he didn't say hello, he said, "Are you excited to be going to Watertown?" I opened my mouth to answer, but when he smiled at me and looked directly into my eyes all I could do was stammer, "No . . . um . . . I mean yes . . . in a way . . . but not . . ." Then I looked down at the dust on my shoes. That's when Nanna said in Italian that "hello" and "yes" would have been enough and added something about a hen being too bold around the rooster, and Poppa said it was all right and that things are different in the West, and Nanna looked fierce and said, *"Americanannate!"* and pointed at John Wilson, and then Momma said something to Nanna and then everybody was upset and talking back and forth, back and forth. All in Italian! John Wilson looked so confused and I kept staring at my shoes and wishing they would go away. Nanna, Poppa, and Momma, not my shoes. Of course, Netta had to say something and I was so embarrassed by it all that I shouted at her, which was a mistake because Nanna started on me. Uncle Eugenio and Aunt Marta and Rosaria came to see what was wrong, and I noticed John Wilson backing away from us — and I don't blame him! — and disappearing into the crowd. I don't even have to wonder what he thinks. He thinks I am a silly little girl with a crazy family! And he is right — about my family! The End. TAV

Tuesday, April 17, and still in Estherville

I was too upset and embarrassed to write anything else yesterday. So I sat in the car by myself wishing I was back on Wooster Street. Then I made the mistake of looking in the Shaker Almanac where it talks about the meaning of the shape of the nose. I found my nose and it said, "Such noses belong to selfish, treacherous, and dishonest people. Avoid such faces if you value your happiness." Do you think John Wilson knows this about my nose too? I do not want to read, write, or think anymore. End. TAV

Tuesday, April 17, 1883 in Estherville

Dear Aria,

Teresa has been very mean. I wanted to write in you yesterday and all she said was, "Go away." When I asked why, she said it was none of my business, and would not say another word. I did not have to read what she wrote to know why she was sad, but that is no reason to keep me from you, is it? But I think she is over it all now. John Wilson was watching the cattle when he saw Teresa in the car and smiled and waved to her as if yesterday had not happened. She waved and smiled back. I know because I was nearby and could see both of them. After John Wilson walked away, Teresa left the car and I was able to find you on the seat. I do not think it is a good thing to leave you out like that. I think John Wilson's smile might have made Teresa forgetful this time. At least it made her forget that she was sad.

I wanted to write about what happened yesterday. The engine that was going to take us to Watertown came right up to us, but before it was attached to the Opportunity cars, the station-master ran out and said something to the engineer. Then the engineer backed his engine up until he came to a long line of cattle cars. There was a lot of loud talk, and even our conductor was angry that the cattle would be moved ahead of us. Our conductor and Mr. Anderson started arguing with the station-master, and a crowd gathered around to listen, but I could not hear. That is when I remembered how Uncle Eugenio told Poppa that people out West act different and are not always polite, and that we had to be like that sometimes if we were going to survive. He did not mean us children, of course, but I decided that this one time it was all right. So I pushed and squirmed until I was right next to our conductor. The cattlemen paid off the station-master and engineer to get the engine. The station-master called it a "special haulage fee," but our conductor called it a bribe and Mr. Anderson said he was going to report it to railroad officials. The station-master didn't care. They were still arguing when I pushed and squirmed my way out and told everyone what had happened. It felt good to be the first to deliver the news. Momma said, "That means we have time to make a nice supper," and I got to help her and taste all the things first.

Yours, Antoinetta

P.S. We did get an engine later — a very old one with a tall smokestack that belched out so much smoke and sparks and fire that Nanna said it must be what the door to hell is like.

Wednesday the 18th

Dear Aria,

Our conductor came into our car and said, "We have just left the state of Minnesota and the United States and have entered the Dakota Territory. We will be at Watertown in no time now." There was a great cheer from everyone in the car, and Ernesto shouted, "I knew it, I knew it," but I don't think he really did. Watertown is the end of the line, Mr. Anderson said, and where our real adventure begins, whatever that means. Netta was upset that I did not say "Dear Aria" yesterday. I did not want to be a "selfish, treacherous, and dishonest" person, so I said I would use it from now on, but I won't put in all of the other things unless they are important. End. TAV

Wednesday, April 18, 1883
Outside the United States of America

Dear Aria,

Teresa said that the farther west we travel, the more I write. I don't think this is true and I am going back through you to prove it. Even if she is right about this, I do not think it is fair that I write less than she does, do you?
Sincerely, Antoinetta

Dear Francesca,

We are almost at Watertown — the very last stop for our train. We will spend 1 more night in this car, but then I will be happy to say good-bye to it and its hard seats forever.

I don't think I asked you how you were in my other letters. Writing in the diary has gotten me used to saying "I" and "me" and not "you" and "yours." I hope your grandfather's toe is better. Momma thinks he might need different shoes because the sidewalks in New York are harder than the dirt roads in Sicily. Has anything changed on our street? I want to know everything — except who is in our apartment. I think knowing that would make me sad all over again.

I have met an interesting boy on the train. His name is John Wilson Anderson and he is 14 — but he looks much older. He says hello to me every time we meet and seems very nice. I will write you more about him when there are no prying eyes around!

1 thing he did tell me was that we would be at Ft. Sully in about 1 month. If you write a letter now, it might be there when we arrive. Can you tell everyone else how to write to me? I can't wait to hear from you.

Love from your friend,

who is now in the Dakota Territory, Teresa

Monday the 23rd

Dear Aria,

I have not had time to write, so much has happened over the last days. We got to Watertown on Wednesday and were met at the station by other people going to Opportunity, including the leader, William Keil. After many hellos and handshakes, Mr. Keil climbed on someone's china barrel to talk.

Mr. Keil is very short — I do not think he is as tall as I am and I am just 5 feet tall — and he was wearing black pants, a black cape, and black hat with a wide, flat brim that a gust of April wind almost blew off his head. I learned later that his only son had died just a few days before, but I did not know it when he first got up on the barrel, so he looked very silly to me. "Friends, friends," he said to get our attention. "I want to welcome each 1 of you to Watertown and thank you for putting your faith in our humble experiment in freedom." He may be short, but he has a big, powerful voice. We could even hear him when our engine chugged and clanked off, and I think the engineer blew the steam whistle extra-long to see if Mr. Keil would stop talking. He didn't. "You are the cornerstones," he continued. "Each and every 1 of you are the foundation, frame, and rafters, the bolts and nails — the *everything* of a new kind of community, where we are equals in every way and where your honest labor earns an honest reward." Everyone cheered so loudly when they heard this that you would hardly know we were tired and grumpy. He told us we would leave for Idaho in about 2 weeks' time, and that every family would have a helper — someone from the Association who is going to Idaho too — to "show you the ropes."

I thought the talk was over, but I was wrong. Next Mr. Keil told us what to expect during the rest of the journey — dusty trails, the bumpy wagon ride, rivers with too much water and prairie lands with too little water. He said these would be difficult and dangerous, "but we can overcome every obstacle because here everyone is your neighbor, and neighbors help neighbors without thought of race, or religion, or reward. That is our only real rule, friends. And that is how you and Opportunity will prosper."

Then Mr. Keil described the land in Idaho. I had read the little brochure on Opportunity and heard Mr. Anderson talk about it, but Mr. Keil made it sound like paradise. "You'll see it first from a mountain-top — a broad valley of hardwood trees and grass and wildflowers with a wide stream of pure, fast-moving water running up the middle. When I say the water is pure, oh, my friends, it's impossible, impossible to describe how deeply sweet and cold and clean it is to the taste. And the soil — 2 feet and more of topsoil so black, so rich with promise that when you smell a handful" — and here he made-believe he had scooped up some dirt and was smelling, then he added — "you'll have no trouble imagining fields of tall corn and wheat, acres on acres, and cabbage and carrots and potatoes. . . ." Poppa was staring at Mr. Keil, a smile on his face — the first I'd seen in a while — and Momma was holding his hand and leaning her head against his arm. Both of them imagining, I guessed. Nanna was also smiling and nodding in approval, and even Ernesto and Netta were actually listening. I had to admit that the scene he was painting sounded beautiful. "It's been there millions of years, friends, waiting, waiting for us to touch it with our plows and axes, our hopes and dreams," Mr. Keil added. "And it is there now waiting for you!" When he finished everyone cheered and clapped. I did too, tho I have to admit I felt guilty, as if I had betrayed Francesca and everyone else back home.

Our helper came the next morning. "Naims Jaims," he said, and he tipped his hat. "'Ceptin' ever-budy colls me Shep." He had to repeat what he said several times before we puzzled it out, and even then Nanna was confused. "What's this about a ship?" she asked Momma in Italian, and when Momma explained that we were to call him Shep, Nanna wanted to know why we needed a shepherd. Of course, Shep had a hard time understanding Poppa's and Momma's American, but Ernesto, Netta, and I were there to explain things.

After this, Shep took Poppa to the stock pens to pick out 2 oxen and a wagon. I volunteered to help everyone understand each other, but Momma shook her head no, and said it was too dusty and rough and that Ernesto would go. Momma made it clear that we had a lot to get ready — *we* meaning the women and girls — and that she needed me, but I wished she needed Ernesto more than me. This time anyway. So *we* packed up everything in the railroad car and left to meet Poppa, Ernesto, and Shep — Netta carrying Tomas, while Momma, Nanna, and I carried bundles of clothes, food, and other things. Later, Poppa and Shep were to go back and get Momma's piano and the bigger things.

Watertown is not very big — a few brick buildings, but mostly small wooden boxes with big signs over the door telling what's sold inside. Some are nothing but tents with wooden fronts. I counted 4 saloons, 1 jail, 3 dry-goods stores, 3 lawyers, 2 barbershops, a bank, 3 blacksmiths, a bakery, 3 boarding-houses, a drug-store, and 4 real-estate offices, plus other stores on some side streets. There was hammering and sawing going on everywhere, so there are probably 2 or 3 more buildings there by now.

We went with Aunt Marta, Rosaria, and the other women from our street, so we made a real parade. 21 in all, counting the babies. Some blocks had wooden side-walks, most didn't, so we marched right up the dirt street, bundles, babies, and all. Everyone in the town stopped to stare and a few pointed and said things, tho I did not hear what, except when 1 man said, "Well, looky here, a reglar herd a eye-tal-yuns."

Momma thinks such people are common and that we should ignore them, but Nanna stared back and kept asking what they were looking at. In Italian, of course, so they just stared harder. All of the stares made me un-comfortable. I noticed how different our clothes and hair and shoes were from theirs, and that our things were soiled and wrinkled from the trip.

Netta didn't seem to notice, tho. She kept on smiling and saying hello to everyone she met, until a group of boys shouted, "Wures yer monkey, girly?" You should have heard what Netta told those boys, and she probably would have gone after them if she wasn't holding Tomas. Aunt Marta said, "That 1 has picked up some bad ways from her sister," and Rosaria nodded in agreement, of course. I felt my face flush, and my mind started to race, but then Momma said, "They speak up for themselves. We could learn something from them." Aunt Marta sputtered, and then she and Momma exchanged words all the way thru town, with Nanna reminding them that they should set a proper example. I didn't listen after a while. I was thinking that Momma had said one of the nicest things about me ever.

We followed a dirt road out of town and met Poppa, Ernesto, and Shep and the wagon in a field near a stream. Our wagon lacks paint and the cover is old and patched, but Shep says it has things that are more important — like wide wheels that won't sink in the soft ground. The 2 oxen snorted and stamped the ground a lot, but they seem gentle otherwise. Poppa also got a milk cow so Tomas will have milk, but it was not a part of the Association agreement so Poppa had to pay $35 extra for it. *"È caro,"* he kept mumbling, so expensive, but Shep said, "Plenty a free grass 'tween her and I-de-hoe, so runnin' her ull be cheep 'nough."

Shep patted our oxen, which are named Zephaniah and Red Top, and said, "Real pullers, both o'um.

An' smart." Shep planned to ride his horse to Opportunity, but if he had a wagon, he said, he would want these 2 oxen to be pulling it. Then he climbed up onto the wagon, took a long stick in his hand, and gently tapped each ox on the rump, barking out, "Come up, boys! Come up! Come up!" Both oxen lowered their heads and immediately started walking forward slowly. After a while, Shep yelled, "Gee! Gee! Gee!" and they turned right without Shep lifting a finger. He went "Haw! Haw! Haw!" and they turned left. Shep marched them around like that for a while — with all of us trooping along — and when he had them back to where he started he yelled, "Whoa! Whoa! Whoa!" and they stopped. Aside from tapping them at the start, he never touched them. And he hardly flicked the reins the way I'd seen drivers in New York do. "See," Shep said after he got down. "Smart'r any horse I know. An' thay don't know me frum Adam. Yur a lucky man, Mr. Vees-car-dee. When they git ta know ya a litle, ya wont even half ta yeall er nothin'." Poppa had such a big smile on his face, you would think he had won a prize.

All through the day, wagons came from town, lining up side by side with enough room between for our tents. The Grosso family is on 1 side of us, the Cardis on the other, with the Orlandos next to them. Uncle Eugenio went on the other side of the Orlandos even tho he could have squeezed in next to us — which I think was Aunt Marta's idea. Later, I counted 54 wagons — white-tops, Shep called them — plus a number of other farm wagons and carts, and spare horses and oxen and beef cattle for the journey. Most people had 4 horses pulling their wagons, Uncle Eugenio among them. Mr. Wilson Anderson came by to see how we were doing, and John Wilson was with him.

Just turned the page and realized it is the last 1 in diary. I, *we*, have almost written you empty and I will try to be — as Mr. Curran says I never am — "brief and to the point."

John Wilson had changed from his traveling clothes into dungarees, boots, a checked shirt, and a wide-brimmed hat. He looked older and I was going to tell him so, but he hardly paid any attention to me. Instead he talked with Shep about the oxen, while Mr. Anderson talked with Poppa about what we needed for the trip. Ernesto and Netta climbed all over the wagon, while Momma and Nanna peered inside and said again and again that it was too small. I had to take care of Tomas and felt left out. I let Tomas pat Zephaniah and told my-self to stay quiet and calm. This is the very end of the

Friday the 27th

Dear Aria,

Found another diary-book at the Chinese store in Watertown. It cost 5 cents. Momma was with me and said that 5 cents was a lot, but the China-man offered to stitch the old and new books together, and then Momma thought the price was fair. Netta says the paper is too thin. I like the yellowy color and the tissuey sound the pages make when they are turned. Anyway, I think it is better to have 1 diary than 2.

John Wilson is acting odd. He says hello and talks with me when we are alone, but whenever Shep comes near, he turns away and ignores me. Maybe it's my clothes or the way I look. Or talk. Oh, I hate thinking these things! It is a waste of time — like writing down the full date at the beginning of every entry. I have decided I won't talk to him whether we are alone or not. It is beginning to rain and Momma wants me to help get things into the wagon. No letters at the post office. Everyone has forgotten me! End. TAV

Sometimes I wish Nanna would — I don't know — leave me alone. I had just finished writing and she asked why I had such a long face, so I told her about not getting any letters and missing my friends from home. All she said was, "Just look around and you might find a new friend or

2." Easy to say, but hard to do — and I told her — and she said, "If you play alone you will never lose," which was her way of saying I'm just scared. Then she added, "Your sister doesn't wear a long face. She goes up and says hello and if she gets a hello back she has another friend. What is so hard about that?" I did not tell her what is so hard about doing that, but I will tell you. Netta is smart and pretty and always says the right thing, and everybody likes her. Sometimes I wish Nanna had stayed in Trappeto! I am going to imagine Francesca writing me a long letter and maybe that will make me feel better. End again. TAV

Saturday the 28th

Dear Aria,

It is raining. Mr. Keil said living out of our wagons until we leave Watertown would give us a taste of life on the trail. So far, it tastes cramped and soggy, with Poppa, Momma, Tomas, and Ernesto sleeping in the tent, and the rest of us stuffed inside the wagon, which is a tight fit because of Momma's piano. And Shep said we haven't even gotten in all of our supplies! Netta wiggles and squirms so. Nanna says it is a sign of a sinful mind, but I think it is just Netta. Already 2 families have decided not to go to Opportunity — and I think they are very smart. John Wilson did not stop by today even tho he said he would, but I am not going to think about him. End. TAV

Saturday, April 28, 1883, from under the wagon

Dear Aria,

I went up and down the line of wagons the other day. Mr. Keil has three wagons and a small coach in which his wife and sister will ride. I learned that from a man who was painting one of Mr. Keil's wagons all black. I said that the black looked sad, and the man told me it would be carrying the body of Willie Keil all the way to Idaho. I decided not to ask the man any more questions. Next I met a girl named Dorothy and I helped her take care of her brothers and sisters. They ran around so much that I could not even count how many there were. Dorothy said that she counted fifteen dogs and eight cats going to Opportunity, plus one raccoon, one snake, one mouse, and two green and yellow birds named Moses and Betty. Tomas is crying.

Sincerely, Antoinetta

P.S. It is good to be writing again.

Another P.S. for Teresa: I am no prettier than you and no smarter (though it is true that I am a better speller). And if I always say the right thing why is it that Momma and Nanna are always correcting me? And I miss my friends from home just as much as you do, only they would want me to have fun, so I do. And if a boy treated me like that I would find another. He does not laugh very much anyway, so what fun can he be?

Sunday the 29th

Dear Aria,

There must be a diary rule that says you can never, *ever* read what someone else has written — even if you know about the Shaker Almanac — and that you should mind your own business, especially about boys! Do you hear?

It is raining hard and our little world is wet, wet, wet — hair, clothes, books, and spirits. Said prayers, helped Momma patch holes in canvas, wrote letters home, said more prayers — to get the rain to stop — helped Momma, helped Nanna, read a chapter from Ernesto's LIVES OF THE PRESIDENTS OF THE UNITED STATES OF AMERICA, listened to Momma play sad songs on her piano. Tomas coughed and cried a lot. Netta named the milk-cow the Empress Christina, but I am still the 1 who has to milk her. No visitors, so I pictured our street on a rainy spring afternoon. That was my day. End. TAV

Dear Francesca,

Why haven't you written to me? I am very lonely and have no 1 to talk to or tell things to. The boy I mentioned — John Wilson Anderson — has not visited in several days. There is nothing to do — except chores! — and think up silly ways to pass time. The other day Ernesto said he was bored, and Poppa went out and bought him a mule to ride — and Poppa did not even complain that it cost $20! When I say I am bored Momma gives me another chore to do. So please write so that I can hear your voice and know that you remember me. I know how much you like the color blue, so I am sending you this flower. I put it inside Ernesto's history book and sat on it during supper to press it. The grass around our wagon is filled with them and they are a favorite of our oxen.

Love, Teresa

P.S. If you were here, I would talk you tired and still have more to say. Write soon!

P.P.S. I am going to write to Mrs. Curran and copy it into the diary with yours. Do you mind sharing space with Mrs. Curran? It will be a short letter.

Dear Mrs. Curran,

We will be leaving here in a few days and I wanted you to know that I am working on my lessons almost every day. In the morning before breakfast, I read and then write out spelling words; next, I try to do numbers and read; later, if there is time, I memorize the spelling and meanings of 5 new words from Netta's dictionary; in the evening, I read geography until there is no light. Momma tests me on my lessons when she can, which is not often, but enough, I think, to be a help. I try to write in my diary whenever I can and I think this practice is helping my penmanship. Will you celebrate May with the singing of the "Flower Song," as we did last year? I will miss that. How are you and how is everyone in class? Are the trees green yet? I did not expect it, but we are in a sea of pale green grass and pretty wildflowers, purple, blue, white, and yellow. I still miss the little trees and gardens at home! I have not received any letters, but Momma said not to worry and that everyone remembers me. Is she right? She thinks the letters are sitting in Pittsburgh or Chicago and that we missed them. Please write.

Sincerely, Teresa Angelino Viscardi

Monday the 30th

Dear Aria,

No rain, and not much that is new. Tomas is sick and Momma is very cross. Poppa and Uncle Eugenio and the other men have gone to meet the train-master and his associates and hear about the journey. Nanna says that every time something needs to be cleaned or swept or mended, the men have a meeting and smoke their pipes and cigars. End. TAV

4 p.m.: What news! I went to town with Nanna to mail letters and on the way met John Wilson, who said hello as if everything was fine. At first I ignored him. I did not even say hello, just nodded. But after walking a ways with him asking what was wrong and me saying nothing, I told him. He apologized right away and kept on apologizing all the way into town and to the post office and all the way back and ended by saying, "I don't know what I'd do if you didn't talk to me." Nanna cleared her throat many times during this trip. I wish she didn't know as much American as she does, but John Wilson didn't seem to notice. He also said I should call him J.W. because all his really good friends call him that. When John J.W. left us, Nanna said, "He is nice boy," in American. Then added, "But . . . mmm . . . but . . . I don't know the American," so she said in Italian, "He apologizes more than a man should." I thought what he said was what he should have said. Momma does not feel well, and I must help Nanna make supper. End. TAV

Tuesday, May 1, 1883

Dear Aria,

    I have made a new friend today named Edith Richardson. She doesn't like the name Edith and will only answer when called Edi. Her family lived near Pittsburgh and she is three inches taller than me. We went around to all the wagons giving out flowers but I was afraid when we came near Mr. Cross's. He always yells at us children when we play close to his wagon. Dorothy says he is cross in name and cross in nature, but Edi did not agree. Even though he was right there, she said, "Are you home, Mr. Cross?" and he said, "Why, yes, Edi, come in," and he was smiling. He said hello to me, and asked me what my name is. We visited awhile and when we left he said we were both very polite and clever girls and, "Please stop by again." I will, too. Learned this verse from Edi:

> Zaccheus he, did climb a tree, his Lord to see.
> The tree broke down and he did fall,
> and he did not see his Lord at all.

I think it as good as any in the Shaker Almanac and I will show it to Teresa.
Yours, Antoinetta

Wednesday the 2nd

Dear Aria,

Poppa is worried about Momma and Tomas. Nanna made Rosaria help with Tomas, which she did with much scowling. Momma is weak, but when she saw Rosaria she tried to get up and would have but Nanna said no and Rosaria stayed. Rosaria was not happy and slammed and banged things til Nanna said that was enough of the slamming and banging. I have been working extra hard so that we will not need Rosaria's help again. Must end and help with supper. End. TAV

6 o'clock: Poppa told Shep about Tomas and Momma, and Shep said something to 1 of the Irish Brigade, because just before supper the 1 named Liam came by with a jar of liquid. He said it was a mixture of milk, pepper, and whiskey and that it should be warmed and sipped all day long to break the fever. Poppa thanked him, and after Liam left, Poppa, Nanna and I sniffed the liquid, which smelled strange, but not as awful as Nanna said. Poppa sipped it cold and called it unusual, but he said he'd had real medicine that tasted much worse. I do not know if Momma had any, but the jar is half empty now. End. TAV

Wednesday, May 2, 1883

Dear Aria,

I did lessons with Teresa. The only word I misspelled was sintellent or scintelant or scintallant, but I do not care how it is spelled since I do not intend to ever use it. After lunch, we played snap–the–whip and I was on the end and was snapped off against a wheel. It hurt a lot and I cried, but not for long. It is not a very good game if you ask me, especially for the one on the end.

Yours, Antoinetta

Thursday the 3rd

Dear Aria,

Momma and Tomas still sick but Rosaria did not have to help us and I think Momma was glad for the quiet. I made breakfast and lunch, and Nanna did not fuss at all about how I did it. J.W. brought news and helped me get water. All the children are to attend a meeting with the train-master, and Netta asked if we should bring a pipe like Poppa. End. TAV

After supper: We met Mr. Joe Bulleau — the train-master — and his crew and he wasn't nice at all. Mr. Bulleau got up to talk and this is what I remember he said:

"Listen up, ok. I don't want ta say this twice. When we leave hare, I'm the boss. No one else. What I say goes and no back-talk. If any of ma men here tells ya ta do anytheng, just do it fast and keep yer mouth shut. We haint got time to nee-go-she-ate, ok?" Then he gave us a long list of don'ts: Don't play on or near the wagons when they're moving because you might fall under a wheel; don't wander out of sight of the wagons because that's how most kids get lost; don't go near any rattle-snakes, coyotes, and wolves no matter how tame they look. And so on. He scared us pretty thoroughly — which is what he wanted to do according to J.W. — and I do not think he will have much trouble with us. While Mr. Bulleau talked, his men — 7 of them — stood behind him looking annoyed and spitting juice. Some-one said they looked like "rough-grained critters" and I have to agree. I do not think water and soap have touched any of them in months judging by the smell that drifted our way when the wind changed directions. After the meeting, Ernesto practiced spitting til Nanna saw him, so he took his mule — which he has named after the famous Indian hunter General O'Brien — and went off to practice spitting in private. Tomas took a lit-tle milk, and Momma sat up but is still weak and dizzy. End. TAV

Friday the 4th

Dear Aria,

Chores, lessons, more chores. Had visitors today: Mrs. Kozwitski and her daughter Katerine (who is 18) and Mrs. Anderson, all bringing something for supper — corn bread, cabbage, and prairie chicken stew, and a very pretty pie. Nanna sniffed at the stew, but it smelled fine to me. Momma seemed pleased by the visit, and Mrs. Anderson even took Tomas — who is much stronger — and said, "How is our little piggywig today," and Tomas giggled like his old self. Must fetch water for washing. End. TAV

Sunday, May 6, 1883

Dear Aria,

Teresa has been awfully crabby and she is not the sick one. After saying prayers, I went with Edi to visit Mr. Cross again and he was as nice as the first time. He is a very interesting man even if he is so old. He drew a map of the world on an egg and told us the names of the seas and even showed us where Constantinople is. He said he lived there long ago when he still had hair on the top of his head, but I am not sure I believe him about either.

Yours, Antoinetta

Monday the 7th

Dear Aria,

You would be crabby too if you had to do chores and lessons while others can spit and play and be served. I will not mention names since it is probably not lady-like, but when I said something Nanna said, "Boys must be boys while they can because soon they will do the work of a man." I think he could be a boy all he wants and still carry a bucket of water. Poppa has gone with some of the other men to get supplies. We are supposed to pack up our wagon as if we were leaving so Mr. Bulleau can inspect it tomorrow morning. I do not like the idea of him looking into our wagon, but we don't have much choice, I guess. End. TAV

Tuesday the 8th

Dear Aria,

Early this morning, we finished packing our wagon til every inch had something in it and something on top of that something til it reached the canvas top. We are waiting for Mr. Bulleau to get to our wagon. End. TAV

7 o'clock in the evening: Momma was so mad. Mr. Bulleau came by and looked at our wagon, all the time shaking his head and making a funny grumbly sound in his throat. Then he said, "Too much. Dam mess'll tip over tha furst little bump," and told us to take out 300 pounds and Momma's piano. He said the same thing about a lot of other wagons, so all up and down the line people were unloading rockers and bureaus and looking sad. But not as sad as Momma! She said her piano reminded her of home — her old home before she married Poppa because that's where she took it from.

Momma must be over her fever, because she did not look at all tired, just angry and stubborn, and she made us unload and load the wagon all morning. She put a trunk of her own and Poppa's clothes off and 2 small rugs, the big pot, and other items, including a suitcase of my Sunday dresses, but I did not care much for them. Mr. Bulleau just shook his head and said more had to go or he wouldn't let us come along. Nanna moved a trunk of her clothes to Uncle Eugenio's wagon, but he said he didn't have room for anything else. Rosaria looked at me and smiled when he said this, but then Nanna told him to make room for our small boxes and he did by putting out a chair — which did not please Aunt Marta — and so my Sunday dresses are coming along. Shep came by and helped Poppa move the big sacks of beans and corn flour and such, but I could tell Poppa was getting impatient because he began mumbling under his breath and shaking his head. Finally, Poppa said there was no other way to pack and nothing else to take off, except the clothes he was wearing, so the piano *had to be left behind,* and Momma said *if it had to stay then so did she!*

Momma sat on the piano stool rocking Tomas and not saying a word to Poppa or anyone. Nanna sent Netta and Ernesto off to play, but I would not leave and she said, "God punishes nosy girls." I do not think that is true. I think God is just as nosy as I am about these things. Poppa asked Momma to tell him what to do, but Momma would not say a word. It was like this for a long while when Mr. Keil and the rest of the Association and Mr. Bulleau appeared and Mr. Keil wanted to know if there was a problem. Poppa said nothing was wrong, that we would have our wagon ready soon. Poppa was so nervous, he said some of this in American, some in Italian. Nanna added that Mr. Bulleau was a bully and worse than the lowest cheating *padrone,* but neither Mr. Keil nor Mr. Bulleau understood, so I explained — about the piano, not what Nanna said. Then a miracle happened. Mr. Keil's eyes opened wide, and he said, "We can't have that, can we? Music is too important to our community, to its spirit." He said the piano could go to Opportunity in one of his wagons. Momma stood up when she heard this and I think she would have kissed Mr. Keil, but of course she didn't. She bowed her head and said thank you several times softly and so did Poppa, and Nanna told Mr. Keil that "God would smile on such a generous heart" (which I repeated in American), tho Nanna also said that Mr. Bulleau would "kiss vipers on the lips for eternity" (which I did not repeat, but I think Mr. Bulleau understood anyway). Mr. Keil bowed to my parents and said a driver would come by for the piano, then he went up and down the line of wagons, offering to take on a favorite chair from 1 family, a small table from another, and so on. When he had no more room, he found others who did. There were still a lot of things that would be left behind, but Poppa said Mr. Keil was a true gentleman and Momma agreed — and I think everyone felt better about going to the Idaho Territory. Now to bed. We leave early tomorrow and Poppa reminded me that I will have to walk most of the way! End. TAV

Tuesday, May 8, 1883

Dear Aria,

Went all around camp today but no one had time for visiting. Not even Mr. Cross. Patted animals and threw stones and Edi swatted a mean ox on the nose when it tried to bite her. Zaphaniah and Red Top would never do such a thing. Mr. Keil's black wagon has a new white cover with a black bow at-

tached to each side. That is the wagon that will lead the train all the way to Opportunity with his son inside. I said it looked scary and that I wouldn't want to be in it alive or dead, but Edi said I was silly and made me climb up inside. Just to see, we lay down in the bed with our arms crossed over our chests and our eyes closed. Edi started to laugh and so did I, and then Edi wondered what Mr. or Mrs. Keil would say if they found us there, so we got out. The wagon Edi is in will be twenty wagons in front of ours. Edi said she would walk a little slow and I should walk a little fast and we would meet in the middle and walk together. I think this is a good plan.
Sincerely, Antoinetta

Wednesday the 9th

Dear Aria,

We are waiting for the train to move, so I will write while I can. Mr. Keil gave the most impressive speech I have ever heard — and I have heard Father Ignatio from Italy preach on Easter morning. Mr. Keil said that at long last the day to leave for the Idaho Territory and our future homes was upon us. He started off slow, but soon his words were coming faster and faster and every part of the trip sounded dramatic. After a while, he asked us all to pray to our own God for safety and clear skies during the trip. Every head was bowed and all was quiet, til

I heard Netta and her friend giggling, but they stopped when Nanna pulled Netta's ear sharply and said something into it that made Netta stand up straight. Mr. Keil ended by pointing up the road: "To the west is the great Missouri River — to the west are the rolling hills of Montana and the noble Rocky Mountains — to the west is the Idaho Territory, a land of plenty, a land of Opportunity! Our Opportunity!" When he said this last part his voice was very loud, and everyone cheered, and a few men even fired off their guns til Mr. Bulleau yelled at them. I have to admit that I felt excited too. We are all eager and happy to be leaving, which is not at all what it felt like to leave Wooster Street.

Later: I am tired, tired, tired — and dusty inside and out. And I only walked 7 miles! Poppa said that Shep said that Mr. Wilson Anderson said that Mr. Bulleau said we would have to do twice that a day and more soon, but I do not think it possible. He also said we are lucky there is a real road to travel on during the first days, tho I don't think this would pass as a real road back home. The 1 time I complained about walking, Nanna said, "The lazy goat is soon eaten by the wolf," but that isn't fair since *she* rode in the wagon all day with Tomas. I would ask if I could have a mule like Ernesto, but Momma would never allow it. End. TAV

Dear Francesca,

Momma thought I looked sad after supper and said I should write my very best friend — and you know who that is. We were up before the sun and moving west before 7 o'clock. The only thing interesting about our wagon train is that the lead wagon is painted black and is carrying a dead boy. The first big bump our wagon hit, Tomas woke and started to complain, but I could hardly hear him over the banging and crashing of pots, the snorts and snuffles of the animals and men, the dry squeaks of the wagons, and such. We were told that the journey would be slow and dusty, but no one said it would be noisy! J.W. — that is John Wilson Anderson — rode up when we had been going a while and got down to walk with me. He told me that the dead boy's coffin is lined with lead and filled with alcohol to keep the body from going bad, but that he doesn't think it will work for long if the weather turns hot. Then J.W. — and this is a secret not to be repeated — took my hand as if we held hands every day! I was so surprised, I almost pulled away, but didn't. I felt my cheeks flush and wondered what Momma and Poppa and Nanna would say if they saw us, but

J.W. was clever and kept his horse between us and the wagon. Mrs. Curran would say this was a "spectacular beginning," and I would have to agree — aside from the dust and walking. Please tell everyone that I miss them and to write.

Love from your friend walking west, Teresa

Thursday noon the 10th

Dear Aria,

Many stops this morning for broken spokes, tired animals, sore feet. Made only 4 miles so far. Mr. Bulleau was angry about the slow pace, but Mr. Keil quieted him by promising that things would go better. That is what J.W. told me. We did not hold hands today. When Nanna saw him, she handed Tomas out of the wagon to me and told me he needed fresh air. Netta pestered J.W. with 100 questions — at least! — and he even let her sit on his horse while he held the reins. I am sure Nanna would have said something about a lady riding, but I think she wanted Netta there to watch me and J.W. End. TAV

Later: 8 miles covered today. Mr. Bulleau went on about the slowness, and Nanna said he was as "hot as an iron on a stove." In Italian, of course. Poppa laughed at this and said Nanna was sounding more and more like a real cowboy, which did not make her happy. Must get water and then Momma is going to show me how to make *stracciatèlla*, tho we are going to use eggs Momma found in a nest this afternoon and not eggs from a hen. End. TAV

Thursday, May 10, 1883

Dear Aria,

Edi and I scouted the train today while the wagons were moving and managed to get yelled at by two of Mr. B's men. One told us we were playing too close to the wagons and to get away. The other said we were too far away from them and to get back. Had walking visits with the Irish Brigade, Mr. Cross, Mrs. Kozwitski, and Dorothy's family (and I managed to count the children this time; there are seven of them). Dorothy had to stay to help her mother. One of Mr. Hesse's horses stepped in a hole and broke its leg. Mr. B shot it and made the other wagons go around while another horse was hitched to the wagon. Edi and I did not think it was right to leave the dead horse right there, so we said a prayer and put purple flowers on it. Edi does not think horses go to heaven, but I do. How would angels get around when they get tired of flapping

their wings? Edi said angels are magical and never get tired,
but if they are magical, why do they need wings to fly?
Yours, Antoinetta
P.S. Teresa has just come back from getting water and she is
wearing that Mr. John Wilson smile.

I was not wearing any sort of smile! I was carrying buckets of water — without any help — and trying not to splash my dress and that is all I was thinking about! If you can't say anything better, then do not write anything at all. It is *my diary* and that is *my rule!* End. TAV

It is Friday morning.

Friday the 11th

Dear Aria,

14 miles today. J.W. visited at mile 6 and then again later. Whoever said this road is flat has not walked it. The road angles up for mile after mile, dips down a while, then rolls along like waves of water. Camp is very quiet tonight. No music and few wasted words. Mr. Bulleau looks pleased and not a bit tired. Netta wants to write something, and I do not feel like arguing. End. TAV

Friday, May 11, 1883

Dear Aria,

　The train moved so fast today that Edi and I had to stay close to the wagons, which was A-O (as some of Mr. B's men shout when something is okay).

　One of Mr. B's men shot a rattlesnake today and cooked it for his supper! Momma said we must all go to sleep now since tomorrow will be a very long day. I asked how one day could be longer than another, but Momma did not want to hear this. Good-night, Antoinetta

Saturday the 12th

Dear Aria,

　Aunt Marta hurt her ankle walking, and Momma was the first to help her. It was not broken, which was a relief to everyone, especially to Nanna, who told us about a neighbor-woman in Trappeto who broke her leg and died a horrible death from poisoned blood. This was not something Aunt Marta wanted to hear, but it did serve to pass time while Momma wrapped Aunt Marta's ankle in a cool wet cloth. We had pulled our wagon over to help and pretty soon the train became a dusty smudge in the distance. Poppa and Uncle Eugenio lifted Aunt Marta into their wagon, and Momma stayed with her to make her comfortable. Aunt Marta seemed very happy to have Momma there, which surprised me very much and I said so, but Nanna said, "This is not your business," but I think it is. A little. Aunt Marta kept telling Momma that she was a saint, and that there would be a special place in heaven for her, that she didn't know how she could ever repay her, tho she would stop every time the wagon hit a hole and yell at Uncle Eugenio for his bad driving. I wonder if this friendliness will last after her ankle is better.

We followed the dust of the train for the rest of the day, which made my mouth gritty and dry. We were so far behind that we could not even stop a minute in the towns of Clark or Raymond, but hurried up the main street. Zephaniah and Red Top were snorting and tired, but we finally caught up with the rest after dark. Mr. Bulleau said we had made 15 miles. So far we have traveled a total of 44 miles. The Shaker Almanac says a mile is 5,280 feet long. If every step I take is 2 feet long, that means I have taken 116,160 steps since we left Watertown! And we are still 600 miles from the Idaho Territory! End. TAV

Sunday the 13th

Dear Aria,

Road fairly flat and smooth — for this road — so Aunt Marta did not complain as much about Uncle Eugenio's driving. At 1 stop I saw a sign near a little trail that cut across the road: PARADISE VALLEY RANCH — IMBERT MILLER III, PROPRIETOR. I went up the trail to the top of a rise to see the ranch. In a gully way off, I saw a tiny, sod house that looked like a packing crate and a shed surrounded by prairie grass and space and nothing much else. I would not say this was a ranch or a valley *or paradise,* but I did see a man cutting long furrows, so I guess I did see Imbert Miller III, proprietor. Came to water at mid-afternoon. Shep called it a creek, but it looked like a river to me, the water was rushing by so furiously. Mr. Keil suggested we stop for the day and go across in the morning when men and animals were fresh, but Mr. Bulleau said no, we had to cross before dark. Luckily, one of his men found a place down-water where the creek widened out and was calmer and not very deep. A rider on each side guided the animals and the water barely came to the hub, so the crossing was not hard at all, tho it took most of the afternoon. 10 miles today, but Mr. Bulleau seems happy anyway. End. TAV

Later: I was cooking supper in the kettle when dark clouds filled the sky and a hard wind started blowing. There was a great hurry to get the wagon tops and tents secured, the animals cared for, and the food cooked before the rain hit. When it did start to fall, it came down in sheets that pounded at the canvas tops and beat the grass flat. Everywhere people scurried for cover, dark shapes lit every so often by blinding flashes of lightning. After dinner, J.W. came over and we — Netta and Ernesto included — watched the storm from under the wagon. We had to huddle together to stay warm and dry and I still remember the warmth of being that close to J.W. On Wooster Street, I would have been inside and dry and warm, but I never would have seen such a wide-open storm, and never would have sat with J.W. I wondered if Imbert Miller III had a family or whether he was sitting alone in his ranch. End. TAV

Monday the 14th

Dear Aria,

Rained all day, but made good time — except at water crossings — and stopped east of Redfield for the night. 16 miles. End. TAV

Tuesday the 15th

Dear Aria,

Raining still, but not as hard. Began crossing the James River at 7. Mr. Hesse grumbled at the price of $3 per wagon and 50 cents per team. After crossing, we left Red-field and immediately met a stage that was headed for Watertown. The road is only wide enough for 1 wagon, so Mr. Bulleau and the stage driver got into an argument over who should move to the side of the road. The stage driver said he had US Mail and the legal right of way. Mr. Bulleau said he had over 50 wagons and did not care about the US Mail. Each man used colorful language to explain his position. Finally, Mr. Keil said we would pull to the side, which did not please Mr. Bulleau, but did end the fight. Made only 9 miles as a result. End. TAV

Wednes

Thu

Friday the 18th

Dear Ar

Saturday the 19th

Dear Aria,

Your pages were too wet to write on these past few rainy days. Finally, I dried you out by the fire. Came to town of Orient — a sad little place of 3 sod buildings and people who do not smile — late Wednesday. Mr. Bulleau said we were behind schedule, so instead of striking out south for Ft. Sully, he headed us west, saying he knew a shortcut that would save a lot of time. When I heard we would not go to Ft. Sully, I almost cried. I was sure there were letters there for me, but what could I do? When many others complained, Mr. Bulleau sent 1 of his men to check for letters.

Travel across the prairie has been steady. The land is like the road — sometimes flat, sometimes not, but it is softer for walking and I suppose it is softer for the animals too. Several of the horse-drawn wagons have fallen behind — including Mr. Wilson Anderson's. Zephaniah and Red Top hardly change their pace, and once yesterday, on a flat section, I saw that Poppa had fallen asleep, but neither animal took notice. Whenever a wagon gets stuck in a soggy patch of prairie, men — including Mr. Keil — surround it and push it clear. So far we have not had to get pushed out of the mud once. Stopped this side of the Okobojo Creek for the night. No sign of the left-behind wagons — or J.W. — but I can see our trail through the grass and suppose they will too. End. TAV

Saturday, May 19, 1883

Dear Aria,

The ground was so wet that Edi and I walked barefoot with our dresses tucked up. I made sure Momma could not see me first. Shep said that Coyote Cal — the man who drives Mr. Keil's black wagon — wouldn't say a handful of words if his pants were on fire. I think a handful means five words in a row, like five fingers, so Edi and I went to see if Shep was right. While we walked alongside the black wagon, I asked Coyote how he was feeling. He said, "Tolerable." Edi asked how the trail was, and he said, "Not bad." I asked how he liked driving a wagon with a coffin in it, and he said, "It's quiet." It went on like this for a while. We were about to give up when Edi asked him how he got the name Coyote. He looked at us and smiled. "Sometimes," he said, "I like ta howl." And he did, right there, with little Willie's coffin behind him! But I didn't care because he had said a handful.

Sincerely, Antoinetta

Sunday the 20th

Dear Aria,

Rained. Papa is sick with a slow fever and needed help driving the wagon. Ernesto was off someplace with his friends, and Shep was helping with the herd, so I got to drive! Momma did not look happy with this, but with the train divided in 2 there was no 1 to spare. Poppa showed me how to hold the reins and what to do and say. I was very nervous at first, but Zephaniah and Red Top do most of the work, and I did not need any help, not even when going down a hill and the brakes had to be used. Poppa said all of my walking has made my legs as strong as his. He didn't say much otherwise, tho on 1 long, flat stretch when Momma and Nanna got out of the wagon to give Tomas some air, he suddenly sighed and said, "Your Momma has given up a great deal to get us to Idaho, Teresa. So much. Her family, her friends, the neighbors . . ." He went on like this for a while, and as he did, I could feel my jaw tighten and my face begin to flush. I was thinking about our street and my friends and my school and how everything in *my* life had been turned upside down and somehow I managed to ask, "What about me?" I must have said it in a whisper because Poppa had to ask me what I said. "Me," I repeated a little louder, my voice shaking. "What about me? It's always Momma this, or Ernesto that, or Nanna or Netta or Uncle Eugenio this and that . . . everyone but me." I wanted to go on and on and tell him how angry I felt inside, but I didn't. I didn't because I could hear my voice getting louder and I remembered how when Aunt Marta gets loud at Uncle Eugenio, Poppa shakes his head disapprovingly and says, "That one shows no respect," and I don't want him thinking the same about me. So instead of saying more, I looked straight ahead and concentrated on driving. "You!" Poppa said in a voice that wasn't scolding but did say I was being silly. "We are doing this for you, and for Ernesto and Netta too. It is a way to make your lives better . . . and that of your children too. And their children. So it is not always so hard." He was quiet after this, and I got nervous thinking he was waiting for me to say something, to say I understood, that it was all right, but it wasn't all right, so I didn't say anything. Finally he sighed and said softly, "In time, Teresa. In time, you will grow up and understand," but I am not sure I will.

10 miles today as we made many stops so the others can catch up — but they are still not in sight. End. TAV

Monday the 21st

Dear Aria,

Another wet day. Poppa told Momma that I would have to drive again because he still feels weak, but then he gave me a little smile. He knows I had fun yesterday. And I think he wanted to make up for our words, to let me know he thinks of me and not just everyone else. Momma wanted Ernesto to drive, but Poppa said the animals knew my voice and ways, and that it would be better not to change drivers. Ernesto went off angry and even Netta was not happy. Nanna said, "A woman who wears pants will 1 day carry stones," but Poppa said it was an emergency. After this, Poppa talked and acted as if yesterday had never happened and that was okay but once when we were on a flat stretch, I said, "Poppa, is it true what you said on the train? That in New York you could not have gotten work?" At first he said I shouldn't be troubling my pretty head with such serious thoughts, but I think he noticed my jaw getting tight again, so he said, "I could have gotten work, yes, even without Eugenio. I could have put food on our table. But many people look down on us because we are from Sicily. Even those from the north in Italy look down on us and call us beasts or worse. That is no way for a man to live." He paused a moment, then added, "That is no way for my children to live. But here and in Idaho we start even, and if we work hard we can get ahead." Then he looked off to the right, water dripping from the brim of his hat, the same hat he wore back in New York on Sundays but dirty from the trail. I wanted to say that I could have helped back in New York, that if he had explained, we could have all gotten jobs, but I knew it would embarrass him to say he could not take care of his family himself, so I didn't. 7 miles . . . and no J.W. in sight. End. TAV

Tuesday the 22nd

Dear Aria,

The sun came up today — after 8 days of clouds and rain!! Saw smiles on everyone, even Mr. Bulleau. Felt good to be walking again too. The land is flat and empty — not a house or tree or anything much in sight all around. Halted after just 8 miles when we saw other wagons. Their animals look all out, and Mr. Bulleau mumbled that we would have to stay here a day to let them rest. I do not think anyone — except Mr. Bulleau and maybe his men — cares if we lose a day. Had a *long* visit with J.W.! End. TAV

Wednesday the 23rd

Dear Aria,

A perfect, restful day with flaps up on wagons and everything outside to dry. Almost like Sunday at home. We learned last night that once across the Missouri River the new route will take us thru Sioux lands. Some people are upset — including Momma and Poppa. And me! Everyone says the Lakota Sioux are a warrior tribe and very fierce. Netta said there is much talk among the children about being kidnapped and made into slaves. J.W. told me his father and Mr. Keil and others are annoyed with Mr. Bulleau, but there does not seem to be much they can do. Changing direction again will mean more lost time. Then J.W. — but I will end here and not say more until I have had time to think about it. End. TAV

Wednesday, May 23, 1883

Dear Aria,

Saw prairie dogs today, but did not tell anyone. I did not want them to end up in a cooking pot. Teresa spent a lot of time getting water with John Wilson. Edi said they are sparking and that we should keep an eye on them. So Edi and I went scouting. When we got near the water, we crawled along until we could see Teresa and John Wilson. John Wilson had already filled a bucket and was handing it to

Teresa, and she was giving him an empty one at the same time. That was when he leaned down and kissed her! As fast as a thought can enter your head! I saw it myself. I think Teresa and John Wilson were both embarrassed. She looked down at the bucket, and John Wilson said they should get back, which is when Edi giggled and I did too, so we got away from there fast. Edi said it wouldn't surprise her if they were married before we reach the Idaho Territory. I do not think Poppa would allow it, but Edi said strange things happen out here.

A rider from Pierre stopped and told Mr. Bulleau that Indians had surrendered at Beaver Creek over in Montana, and that some were killed near Wild Horse. Mr. Bulleau looked upset and asked many questions, but the rider did not have any more news about this. He did say that there were now electric lights in Cheyenne and Denver, but Mr. Bulleau did not seem interested in this at all.

Sincerely, Antoinetta

Thursday the 24th

Dear Aria,

We are at the Missouri R, tho it looks more like a big muddy lake to me! We arrived late in the morning, and Mr. Bulleau said it would take 3 or more days to get all of the wagons, people, and animals across — with the help of the Indians! There was a lot of talk when that was announced. Momma looked frightened and when she told Nanna, Nanna made the sign of the cross. Mr. Hesse said we should go south to Ft. Sully and cross there, but Mr. Bulleau said no. There was a trail on the other side that would take us across Indian land straight to Montana and Idaho and it would save us time. Mr. Keil and the rest of the Association called a meeting with Mr. Bulleau to talk over the route. Poppa said they should have talked over the route before we got here, and Uncle Eugenio said we could find Ft. Sully on our own and get another guide there. But 1 of Mr. Bulleau's men said we should stop our bellyaching. "He's parta thair family," he said, meaning Mr. Bulleau. "His squaw's tha daughter of a big muck-a-muck over thare. Aint nothin' gonna happen ta nobody 's long 's Bulleau's 'round." Shep and some others seemed happy to hear this, but most were not. I am not so sure. So far Mr. Bulleau has known where there is drinking water and easy places to cross the streams. But being surrounded by Indians is another matter. Tho it is probably not as bad as having a nosy little sister following you around all the time. End. TAV

Later: It is settled. We will follow Mr. Bulleau's route — Indians and all. Neither Poppa nor Uncle Eugenio are happy about this, but they do not want to leave the train and be on their own. 2 families are turning back, and 1 of Mr. Bulleau's men is taking them to a town a long day's journey from here. Mr. Bulleau has gone to get the Indians and then we will begin crossing. End. TAV

Thursday, May 24, 1883

Dear Aria,

It is not fair! Dorothy's parents have decided to turn back. Mr. Wagor said we would be outnumbered and at the mercy of the savages. Sometimes I felt this way on Wooster Street because most of the people were from different parts of Italy from us, and there were so many Irish and German families there too. But it did not keep me from playing outside. Edi said we could hide Dorothy in a box and Dorothy's family would not miss her right away. I think they would know she is gone. Dorothy has a very loud voice and she is not shy about using it. We are trying to think up another plan.
Sincerely, Antoinetta

Friday the 25th

Dear Aria,

We spent all day gathering wood — there are a lot of trees near the river — washing clothes, cleaning the wagons, fixing spokes and such. The stock caught up with us and several cattle have been butchered and Mr. Keil says we should celebrate tonight, tho he did not say what we are to celebrate. I am going to write Francesca and send it back with the Wagor family. End. TAV

Later: At dusk we saw fires and activity on the other side of the river. 1 of Mr. Bulleau's men said the Indians would begin cutting trees and lashing together rafts in the morning. The animals will go across a day before us so they are ready for us when we arrive west-river. End. TAV

Dear Francesca,

We are at the Missouri River but not at Ft. Sully. We are somewhere above Ft. Sully across from the Sioux Indian lands, and *they* will be helping us cross the river!!!! J.W. thinks everything will be fine because the Indians are getting $1 a wagon for the crossing — which is much cheaper than at Ft. Sully — and another 50 cents to go on their land, and besides that they do not want any trouble with the army. Momma and Poppa still don't like the idea. Poppa said he would keep the rifle near him every minute, with bullets in his pocket. Momma told us to wear our hair up under our bonnets and not look at the Indians for any reason. Nanna thinks we should all stay inside the wagon the whole time, but Poppa said we would have to leave too many things behind if we did that. Oh, how I wish I was back home with you and not here worrying about river crossings and Indians and wolves. The 1 good thing is that there has not been 1 argument — not a real 1 anyway — between any of us, which Nanna says is the work of Saint Jude and the bottle of holy water she brought all the way from Trapetto. I have more — much more — to say on this particular subject but

Still Friday

Dear Aria,

Letters! Letters! Letters! The rider from Ft. Sully has brought a bag of letters, and 2 of them are for me!!! 1 is from Mrs. Curran and the other from Francesca. Momma and several others from our street have also received letters and we are to share news tonight after supper. I will read my letters myself, then paste them in this diary for safekeeping. End. TAV

April 26, 1883
My Dear Teresa,

What a wonderful surprise to find your letter waiting for me when I arrived home yesterday. I was sorry to hear that you had not gotten the letter I sent to you via General Delivery at Pittsburgh. I can only guess that the heavy rains delayed it until you had passed through. It rained and rained and rained after you left, one day after another, until I thought I would need an ark to get to school. Emma Durant said the sky must miss you as much as we do and that it is crying.

One thing the rain did was clean away all of the dirt and debris left by winter, so that our streets and buildings seem to sparkle, they are so clean. The water must have also helped the trees and plants because they seem particularly active this year and promise abundant flowers and foliage.

Yes, we did have a May Day pageant complete with the singing of the "Flower Song." Mary Taylor filled in for you and did an admirable job, though she does not have your dramatic flair. At the end of the

performance, Annie Nolan recited a special poem she had written about you called "Gone Is the Friend." It was well received, and many a tear was shed. Annie said she sent it to you in a letter, but I am enclosing a copy of it here in case the letter never reached you.

We have been following the progress of your journey very closely. Each time one of your letters arrives, we note the location and place a colored pin in the map to mark your route. You seem to be making rapid progress, and we are all very eager to hear more about your trip. When you have time, would you send a letter to the class telling us all about your experiences and about the people you meet on your trip? There is much discussion here about the Indians, and I am sure your classmates want to hear about your encounters with them.

I was glad to learn that, despite the many difficulties of travel, you are pursuing your studies so diligently. It may be impossible to imagine, but everything you learn now will be of use to you throughout your lifetime. My father, who had traveled widely and was a learned man, used to say, "An empty mind is Satan's slate," which is very true. But an empty mind is something even sadder, if that is possible. It is like a bureau whose drawers and compartments could hold so much that is dear and valuable, but instead remains bare and hollow. As our friend Mr. Thomas Hill writes in his MANUAL, "Boys and girls should store their minds with knowledge, whereby they may be able to impart the knowledge which they possess; and those who store the mind in youth with valuable knowledge, will possess that which can never be lost, but on the contrary will always be a means by which they may procure a livelihood; and, if united with energy and perseverance, will be sure to give them reputation, eminence of position, and wealth." These are important words to remember, especially when a particular lesson seems difficult or challenging.

Please remember me to your family. I shall anxiously look for a letter from you in the very near future. I remain your teacher and friend,
Mrs. Charles B. Curran

GONE IS THE FRIEND
BY ANNIE ELIZABETH NOLAN

Gone is the friend
We held so dear,
Gone to broad valleys
With streams so clear.
She travels far roads
And steep mountain trails,

Leaving brave footsteps
In green, grassy vales.
Her name is oft spoken
With happy recall,
Her laugh echoes still
Through these long, learned halls.
And while she is gone
Our spirits can soar,
She lives in our hearts
And our minds evermore.
May your journey be swift,
May you ever be well,
So farewell, dear friend,
Farewell. Farewell.

Dear Teresa,

We all want to hear more about your J.W. Anderson. How tall is he, what color are his eyes and hair, is he handsome, is he nice, does he ride a horse well? Nicola especially wants to know about this last one. Annie overheard Nicola and I talking about you and J.W. one day and she said you were probably making him up, but we said you would never do that and that you always told the truth — unlike some girls we know. When I said this I was looking right at her so she knew exactly who I meant. Then Annie went and wrote a poem about you that she read at the pageant, and Nicola and I thought we would be sick, it was so awful — not in what it said about you, but because Annie was saying it. I couldn't listen to her, so I can't write it down for you, but I do remember that at the end she made a dramatic wave with her hand and said, "So farewell, dear friend,/Farewell. Farewell," and Anthony made a rude noise as punctuation. Everyone laughed — even Mrs. Curran, though she tried not to show it — and Anthony was so proud of his performance, I thought he was going to take a bow with Annie. If you had been there you would have laughed until your sides ached because mine did. It served Annie right anyway. So send more news about your J.W. and I will be sure Annie hears about it.

Mother just told me to end my letter and go to sleep. Everyone misses you terribly — especially me! I keep all of your letters under my pillow and I read them every night. Really! Well, almost every night. I hope this letter gets to you so you know that I am thinking about you. Father Dominic sends his best to your family and says that his prayers are with you. Mr. Simeti's horse died — just fell over cold dead the other morning, and no one knows why. They have begun to dig up the street, but, like Mr. Simeti's horse, no one knows why! There is so much I want to say —

but Mother is getting impatient, so all I have time to say is: Farewell, dear friend,/farewell/if you don't say your prayers/you'll fall down a well!
Love from your best friend, Francesca

Francesca,

I stopped writing in the middle of the last sentence because your letter and Mrs. Curran's just arrived and I couldn't wait to read them. It was so good to hear your voice after so long. How long has it been? So long I can't even count the days! Now you must write even more and send it to the post office in Lemhi in the Idaho Territory. I do not know what towns we will stop at between here and the Idaho Territory, but promise you will write. Please.

I must help Momma with supper and then I am to read my letters to the others from our street — with great care to leave out certain parts. Tomorrow, a family going to Gettysburg 20 miles east will take this letter, and I only wish I could fold myself up small enough to fit inside! As for J.W., you can tell Annie that he holds hands *and* kisses very well! He also rides a horse very well. Be sure to let Nicola know that.

Love, Teresa

P.S. Nothing is worse
   Than to be praised in verse
   By a person who never is nice.
   But a letter from you
   Who has always been true
   Is like having spring flowers bloom twice.

Monday the 28th

Dear Aria,

I can hardly believe how much I have talked these past days. Her name is Mary Margaret Degler and she is a friend of Katerine Kozwitski, but younger by 3 years and closer to me in age. We started talking and discovered we had many things in common — her father is strict like Momma, she has a pesky little sister who also manages to avoid most chores, her grandmother is with them and always has something to say about everything, tho her grandmother begins her advice with "in our village," which Nanna has not yet said. And more. We talked and talked and it was almost as if I was with Francesca again. I even told her how I worried I would never have a friend my age and she said she had the same feeling! It is strange how 1 thing can lead to another and another. If Momma hadn't gotten sick and if Mrs. Anderson hadn't arranged to bring supper over with Mrs. K and the others, I never would have met Katerine and then I never would have met Mary Margaret. Momma is even happy that we are friends. She said now that we are to go across Sioux lands it will be good to do chores in pairs for protection. And when I wasn't talking with Mary Margaret I had J.W. to talk with. I am near talked out, as Shep would say. The Indians have been hard at work. The river is very wide here, but we can still see them moving along the banks chopping down trees and hauling them to the water. End. TAV

Wednesday the 30th

Dear Aria,

We are now west-river, safe and sound. This morning the Indians paddled the rafts across to us, making much noise as they did. Mr. Bulleau was with us and said everything was fine, otherwise I think most would have run away out of fear. J.W. said he counted 58 Indians, but it seemed like many more to me. When they were closer, we could see they were very handsome with light brown skin, thick, dark hair, and well-muscled in the arms and chest. Some had on hardly any clothes at all! Momma told us not to look at them, and I did as I was told, except for quick glances from under my bonnet. Just before they landed, we got into the wagon and I did not see much after this — not with Tomas demanding attention and Nanna, Netta, Ernesto, and I stuffed between the piano, sacks of flour, bedding, furniture, and boxes and hardly any air. Poppa helped the other men on the raft, and Momma sat on the spring seat and talked to us during the whole crossing.

We were to the front of the train, so we went early. 6 men pulled us on and stayed to steady the wagon during the trip and haul it off on the other side. The raft was pushed out, and the Indians and men began paddling — with all kinds of accompanying whoops and calls. The raft bobbed and bucked in the water, then spun around and bobbed and bucked some more — and my stomach did too. Nanna tried to get us to say prayers to the Little Madonna for a safe crossing, but every time the raft lurched up or sideways the words stuck in my throat, so I never said 1 start to finish and do not know whether prayers like that work. Netta kept peeking out from under the canvas and giving us little reports on what she saw, but 1 time she had just put her eye close when 1 of the Indians let out a howling whoop that made Netta scream and fall over backwards until her dress was over her head. A second later, everyone was laughing — even Poppa and Momma — and 1 of our men said, "I believe the young'un has got an eyeful." Netta yelled that it wasn't funny at all, but she got another war whoop as an answer and more laughter. I even saw Nanna smile. I did not say it but I thought she got what a nosy person deserves, if you get my point.

Getting across took a long time, maybe even an hour, tho I am probably wrong since my head and stomach were bobbing and bucking so much. On the other side, we were dragged up the embankment to Zephaniah and Red Top, who pulled us to a large clearing in the trees where the other wagons were waiting. Poppa unhitched Zephaniah and Red Top, then went back to the river to help others with their crossing. When I stepped down from the wagon, my feet went all wobbly and I had to grab on to Ernesto. He grumbled, but I think that was because Momma told him to stay and help set up camp. Mary Margaret is not here yet, so I thought I would write this and then do chores and lessons — lessons I have ignored for 3 straight days! Saw movement in the woods and thought coyotes had found us. Later, I saw that some of the Indian children were watching us, tho they seem afraid and keep their distance. End. TAV

Wednesday sunset: It all happened so quickly. Every so often we would hear the calls and whoops as a raft neared the riverbank, followed by quiet when they landed. Then a while after, a wagon would pull into the clearing, and another series of calls and whoops could be heard down by the water as the next raft approached. We had gotten used to the sounds of the arrivals, 1 after another, when there was a change. The usual calls and whoops began and were increasing in volume when they stopped of a sudden and everything went quiet for a second or 2. Then we heard hoarse shouts and commands. I recognized 1 voice as Mr. Bulleau's: "Help'm! Help'm! Get out thar now!" he screamed. "Quick, ya dam . . ." I looked to Momma and could see she heard the same thing in the panicked cries. The few men and many women who were in the clearing were already running back to the river and so did I. Momma called for me to stop and said Ernesto would go, but I kept going because Mary Margaret and J.W. were not in the clearing yet and I needed to find out about them. That's when Momma ordered Ernesto to run back with news about Poppa, and I felt bad because I hadn't even thought about him.

When we got to the river, I told Ernesto to look for Poppa while I searched for Mary Margaret and J.W. All down the river there were Indians and men floating in the water, trying to get closer to the shore or holding on to tree roots while others on land waded out to help them. Ropes were being tossed out too. Hardly anyone could swim, so everyone splashed around a lot in the water. I saw a wagon floating wheels-up way down-river caught in a tangle of tree roots with a few Indians and men clinging to it. I heard a woman nearby say that everything was going just fine, then a rope broke and the raft fell apart and the wagon went over, just like that, upside down. I shuddered when I thought about how we had been jammed in our wagon and how it would feel to have everything turned upside down and be under water.

1 of Mr. Bulleau's men came over and told us to get back to the clearing. I said no we were looking for our Poppa and he said he didn't care, get away before he got angry, and I said no again and he took a step in our direction and looked as if he was going to hit me. Ernesto hid behind me, but I didn't move. "Our Momma said to find Poppa and we won't leave til we do!" and that stopped him. But he did yell some more at me about there being dead and injured and not getting in the way. Next, I saw Poppa and Uncle Eugenio and Mr. Grosso pulling an Indian in with a rope and I sent Ernesto running back with the news.

It didn't take long to get everyone out of the water. The woman who had seen the accident didn't know whose wagon had gone over, but 1 of our men appeared and said it was the Hesse wagon. I didn't see Mr. Hesse or his wife or children and began to worry. Mr. Bulleau's man had mentioned dead but not who. Closer to where we were a group of men lifted someone from the water. I saw his head moving, so at least he was alive. It turned out to be Seamus, of the Irish Brigade, who was on the raft when it broke apart and had his leg crushed between the logs. By the time Ernesto returned, I had seen the other men from our street and I told him to go back with this news. He said he wouldn't, that it was my turn, but then I hit him in the shoulder hard and he went off saying he was going to tell Momma. But I didn't care. Not much anyway. Poppa and Uncle Eugenio and the others from our street were alive and it wasn't Mary Margaret's or J.W.'s wagon upside down in the cold water.

After this I sat on the grass and waited. I wanted to see my friends to be sure. Ernesto came back and told me I was in trouble and then would not stay with me, but went off to be with the other boys. I heard later that both Hesse children — Hildi, who was 10, and her 1-year-old baby sister, Caterina — had drowned in the wagon, trapped under boxes and bedding. I had seen both girls before, but only remembered that Hildi had big, dark eyes and always seemed to be sad and quiet. When I thought of this, I wished I'd gone over and said hello to her.

The crossings resumed after a while, and eventually Mary Margaret's wagon appeared. She seemed surprised when I rushed to hug her, but when I told her about the awful accident I think she understood. She told me the Anderson's wagon wouldn't be over for a long while. Mr. Anderson and J.W. were helping people board on the other side and their wagon would be 1 of the last. We walked to the clearing together, and Momma didn't scold me about hitting Ernesto, even tho he reminded her about it. She did ask me not to hit him as hard in the future. When she heard that 1 of the Irish Brigade had been injured she sent Ernesto over with our supper, including the biscuits, and Nanna sent along a bottle of *rosòlio àgli Agrumi,* saying, "Tell him to take a glass or 2 and he will feel no pain."

The camp is very quiet and sad tonight, and we had to make do with a cold supper of leftovers. But that is okay since I kept picturing poor Hildi's sad eyes and wondering if we could have been friends. End. TAV

Thursday the 31st

Dear Aria,

Hildi and Caterina were buried today. Mr. Keil offered to carry them to Opportunity in Willie's wagon, but Mrs. Hesse said she wanted to know they were safe in the ground. Mr. Wagner, who was a clock maker in Cambridge, Massachusetts, made 1 oversized casket so the girls would be together, and everyone said it was finely made considering how quickly he did it. The wood came from one of Mr. Keil's wagons.

Late in the afternoon, we gathered in a quiet part of the woods not far from a stream, and the casket was put into a hole the men had dug earlier. Just about everyone was there, including the Indians, tho they stayed apart from us. Mr. Bulleau's men and some of ours — J.W. among them — were bringing the rest of the cattle and animals across. There are no priests or preachers in the train, so Mr. Keil read prayers from THE BIBLE and said a few words. "Friends," Mr. Keil began, but his voice cracked and he had to stop for a little while. "Friends, no words I say can heal the pain or ease the unimaginable sorrow felt by Caterina and Hildi's loving parents here. And no one knows why these 2 innocents were chosen. It had to be that God missed their gentle smiles and kind natures so much that He —" His words stopped right there, and he glanced down as a terrible quiet filled the woods. "— that He called them to His side for all eternity." He said more, but I found myself thinking about how things seem to happen for no reason and that it could have been us just as easily.

Later, I said this out-loud. Poppa said I shouldn't worry, and Nanna said thinking about worry brings it on, but I couldn't stop thinking about it.

On the way back to the wagons, Uncle Eugenio said, "Did you see those savages? Stood like statues and didn't say or do a thing. Didn't even look sad and they killed those girls." Poppa said he wasn't sure the Indians actually did anything to hurt the girls, but he thought Mr. Bulleau should have checked the rafts every time 1 crossed. I don't know about this. Plenty of our men were on the raft and they didn't see it coming apart, so how would Mr. Bulleau? End.TAV

Later: The Indian drums went on for a long time tonight and it was hard to sleep. We heard the first drum go boom just as the sun went down, then there was a long pause, then another loud boom. Another pause, another boom, again and again, so slow at first that I could count to 4 or 5 between them. Pause — 1-2-3-4. Boom. Pause. Boom. Pause. Boom. Next, the sound of a man's voice, almost like a wailing moan, began to drift to us through the trees. Uncle Eugenio said, "Don't those savages have any respect?" Ernesto asked if they were going to attack. Poppa said don't be silly, but I saw him take bullets from his pocket and load our rifle. Other voices joined the first and the singing and drumming went on, tho louder and at a slightly faster pace. Boom. Boom. Boom. Boom. One of Mr. Bulleau's men said that the Indians were singing and drumming for the spirits of the dead girls, so they would not wander lost in the world. Both Momma and Nanna blessed themselves when they heard this, and Uncle Eugenio muttered, "Haven't they done enough," but I thought it was nice that they cared. A few people from the train went over to see the drumming, but not many. After a while, the pace of the drumming got faster and the singing louder. It went on hour after hour, and Poppa said there was plenty of wood around so I could keep the fire going and write and listen. J.W. came over smelling like Zephaniah after pulling for a day, but I didn't mind since we sat very close, listening and thinking. At one point, Mr. Keil appeared, a little to our right, and walked beyond the wagons until he was close to the line of trees. He stared in the direction of the singing, looking so tired and sad and maybe wondering if establishing a new kind of town was worth 2 dead. "Do you see?" J.W. whispered, pointing toward Mr. Keil. It was dark and I wasn't sure what I was looking for, and then Mr. Keil turned his head some and I saw the shiny trail where tears had run down his cheek. Then, all of a sudden, the drumming and singing stopped and what followed was the quietest quiet ever. For the first time, I noticed how chilly the breeze was. I shivered and so did J.W. and he put his arm around me. J.W. went to say something, but the words got stuck, he was so sad. The only sound after this was the crackle-pop of the fire. Not even the animals made noise. End. TAV.

Dear Aria,

It has been many days since I wrote in you. That is because I did not have anything to say. Now I do. Last night, after Momma and Poppa went to sleep, I left the wagon to meet Edi. Teresa was awake, so I told her that I was going into the woods for nature's call — which I did do — but she was with her J.W., so I don't think she cared where I went. I met Edi near a trail that led to the Indian camp, which is a long walk from the clearing. We were scared, especially when we got close enough to see the fire and the shapes of people. But we kept very quiet and crept up on them without being noticed. They had a great bonfire, which made everything — faces, bodies, clothes, trees, and grass — glow a warm yellow-orange. Most of the Indian men were sitting around the fire, some hitting drums and the rest singing, tho Edi thought it sounded more like the sounds of coyotes howling. Some Indian women were there too and a few children, but most of the children were asleep. I saw Mr. Cross and a few other men from our group, which made me feel safer. I did not know Hildi very well. She was older, and her parents did not let her play very much. So I was surprised at how sad the drumming and singing made me feel, and I think Edi felt the same way because I saw her wipe away a tear. Then Edi yawned, and so did I, so we went back and only got lost for a little bit. Teresa looked at me crossly and said I should be asleep. I just said I wasn't and climbed back inside. I listened to Teresa and John Wilson whispering until Nanna started to snore.

I am your Indian scout, Antoinetta

Friday the 1st

Dear Aria,

The train left early today with no sign of the Indians. There was a rough, narrow trail cut through the trees and we were told army supply wagons sometimes use it. Walking hard today and even riding looked painful the way Momma and Poppa bounced on the spring seat. I wondered how Seamus's broken leg did on such a broken trail. Made just 8 miles. End. TAV

Saturday the 2nd

Dear Aria,

Hard day. Wagons had to be pulled and pushed up 2 stony hills, which took many hours and much cursing. Some grumbling about the route, and a number of men — Uncle Eugenio included — complained to Mr.

Keil, who said something to Mr. Bulleau, who said the trail is flatter once we are beyond the woods. I am not sure this reassured many. J.W. helped with our wagon and walked with us a while after. Later, I walked with Mary Margaret. She said people — her father included — are very angry with Mr. Bulleau and the Indians about what happened to the Hesse girls and about this trail, and not happy that Mr. Keil has not done anything. I asked her what Mr. Keil was supposed to do and she said she did not know. End. TAV

Sunday the 3rd

Dear Aria,

Trail rocky and slow, but we made 12 miles and Mr. Bulleau looked pleased. The sun made the day hotter and Poppa had me drive the wagon some so he could rest. Nanna grumbled about the weather, that it is icy cold in the morning, melting hot in the afternoon. "It can never make up its mind," she said. I reminded her of the days last September when she said the weather was perfect, But Nanna insisted that she has never, ever felt a perfect day in the United States. When I told her we were not in the United States, she said I was being fresh and that in her village children speak with respect to their elders and never, ever point out their errors. But I was giggling by the time she finished, and later, I ran to Mary Margaret's wagon to tell her Nanna said "in our village," and when I did we both laughed and *her* grandmother said "in our village girls control their behavior in public." But neither of us could, and for an instant it felt like I was with Francesca back home. I felt guilty for feeling this way, which is silly because I am sure Francesca would not be upset. I can see J.W. heading this way and will end. TAV

Sunday, June 3, 1883

Dear Aria,

Edi and I made walking visits today. We started with Coyote Cal, then went to Mr. Cross's. He told us all about India and Tibet and about mountains so high, no one has ever climbed to the top. Next, I asked Mrs. Grosso to tell us about I Morti. Early in November there's a holy day called All Souls' Day by the Church, but everyone in Sicily calls it I Morti, which means The Dead. At night on I Morti, all of the dead come out of their graves and wander through the town looking for boys and girls. If the child has been good and has said prayers for the dead, they receive a toy or a sugar statue. Edi wanted to know what happened to bad children, and Mrs. Grosso crossed herself, and so did Edi but she is not Catholic so she crossed herself backwards. Mrs. Grosso said, "I knew one

girl who never said a prayer for her dear dead uncle, not one, ever, even though he had been very kind to her and her family. On I Morti her dead uncle came right to the girl's bedroom, where she was hiding under the bed. "Will you remember me now?" Edi's eyes were very wide when she heard this, and after we left, Edi said she was going to be sure to say a prayer every night for the two Hesse girls, because she would hate to have them follow her all the way to the Idaho Territory. I will say a special prayer for the Hesse girls too.
Sincerely, Antoinetta

Monday the 4th

Dear Aria,

Mr. Bulleau said we were behind schedule, so we struck camp early — and had cold meat, bread, and milk for breakfast. Left the woods a little after noon, but the trail through the grass is not as smooth as some hoped. 1 of Mr. Bulleau's men said if you want government roads you should have stayed home. I drove a little, but walked alongside Zephaniah most of the afternoon, and Mary Margaret accompanied me. She is such a kind friend. J.W. is to tend the herd tonight. End. TAV

Tuesday the 5th

Dear Aria,

Same as yesterday, only hotter. Mary Margaret and I walked and talked together, and then J.W. came riding up. He wanted to know what "you girls are chattering on about," and Mary Margaret said we *girls* were not *chattering on* about anything! I think J.W. did not like the way she spoke to him because he grew quiet and then left. I felt very strange about this and I suppose J.W. is angry at me too for not saying anything. I did not think what he said was *so* bad, but there was something about the way he said *girls* and *chattering* on that did bother me. A little. But I was not sure how to say all of this and not have both of them angry at me. I was thinking all this over when Netta started complaining about Nanna. Poppa told Netta that she had to gather sticks, wood, bones, or boards she found along the trail and put them in the wagon for our fires. But every time she throws a piece in, Nanna yells at her. I was going to chase her away when I had an idea and told Poppa. At our next stop, he took a piece of canvas and nailed it under the wagon, leaving it loose in the middle. Now Netta can run up to the wagon and toss what she finds into the sling without bothering Nanna. Poppa saw it loaded with things to burn and told me it was a very clever

idea, and Momma and Nanna agreed. Imagine that!
End. TAV

Wednesday the 6th at noon

Dear Aria,

Another hot day and little water. A few wagons could not keep up and had to drop out of line to follow as best as they could. We have stopped to rest and feed the animals, tho Zephaniah and Red Top look impatient to be going. Shep thinks they must smell water up ahead. Shep is going to ride with the stock animals and he invited Ernesto to help him. Poppa said it was okay and the 2 rode off — Ernesto going thumpity-thump on General O'Brien and holding his hat from blowing off. I could see that Momma was not pleased with this, but she did not say anything. The call has been made to start again. End. TAV

5 o'clock: Much excitement. Indians — 8 of them — were seen far off to the north following the train. Mr. Bulleau did not recognize them, and rode out toward them, but they did not want to speak to him and disappeared instead. Mr. Bulleau called a meeting and told us they were probably just curious, but then he ordered everyone to be on the alert, assigned extra guards for tonight, and sent riders back to make sure the trailing wagons are safe. Everyone is nervous now. Momma made Netta and I stay near the wagon and is upset that Ernesto is not in her sight. Netta is upset because now she cannot escape doing chores. No visitors today. End. TAV

Later still: Mary Margaret visited. Her mother — who is not so strict as her father — said she could come as long as she stays inside the circle of wagons. She brought a book called JOHN HALIFAX, GENTLEMAN, and we took turns reading it aloud by the fire, tho we laughed more than read because the story and people are so silly. Nanna said we sounded like chickens in a barnyard and that an Indian would hear us and head straight for us like a fox to gabbling geese. Mary Margaret said if that happened she would hit him on the head with her book and that would give him food for thought. Nanna did not understand the joke, but she did say, "Good, and give him a hard hit for me, and 1 for Baby Tomas and Antoinetta, and your fellow goose too." End. TAV

Thursday, June 7, 1883

Dear Aria,

    Teresa said I could carry you today (though she did not look happy about it). Edi and I went up and down the train and asked people what was the silliest name they had ever heard. A few people thought it wasn't a nice question to ask or suggested we say prayers for our safety instead. Mr. Cross laughed when we asked him and said he had once met a man named Rufus Griswold. He said Rufus Griswold is not such a funny name except that he operated a gristmill in the town of Grindstone, Maine. Mr. Cross said the phrase Griswold's Gristmill of Grindstone has never left his head since. Mrs. Anderson said there were two brothers near her father's farm named Erwin and Erastus Beadle. Then we met Mr. Keil walking toward the front of the train. He has been very quiet and sad-looking since Hildi and Caterina drowned, and I did not want to bother him, but Edi just went up to him with our question. I worried he might be very stern, but he wasn't. He smiled a very big smile and said he once knew a man named Thurlow Weed. "The man didn't have any weeds on his entire property. Not a one. Not in the cornfields, not in the vegetable garden, not in the flowerbeds. There was only one weed on the place and that was Thurlow Weed himself!" I am not sure this story is true, but Mr. Keil was nice to tell it to us and it was good to see him smile again. Here is a list of some of the other names we heard: Eldon Draime, Esmerelda Blomp, Heavenly

Farmer, Holden Hat. One of Mr. Bulleau's men said he had met an Indian called Big Hat on Small Head, but did not know why since the man had a regular-sized head and hat. Edi's grandmother said we should stop making fun of people and that everyone on our list would probably think our names were very silly. So I added our names to the list just to show that we were not being mean. Teresa wants you back, so I will close.

Sincerely, Antoinetta

Thursday the 7th

Dear Aria,

Indians appeared again and followed until Mr. Bulleau went out to talk. J.W. rode up and I was about to say something about the other day — to explain why I had been quiet and what I was feeling — when he asked, "Is *she* going to stop by soon?" I did not like the question, but tried not to be angry. *She* may, I said, and I asked if that was a problem. J.W. looked annoyed and wanted to know why she didn't like him. I told him that wasn't true, but that Mary Margaret didn't like when he said we were chattering girls. "That's silly," he said. "I didn't mean anything by it. She can't be very smart if she didn't know that." "She has a name — Mary Margaret — and I guess you think I'm silly and not very smart too because

I didn't like it either." J.W. swallowed hard and was about to say something, but all that came out was um and ah and that I wasn't being fair. Poppa coughed then, I think because both our voices were getting loud. J.W. glanced at Poppa, then back at me, and then he turned his horse and rode off in a hurry. I was angry with J.W., but I was surprised when he rode off so suddenly. And hurt. And annoyed with myself that I had gotten angry. Why can't I control my temper the way Mrs. Curran tells me to? Now he probably won't ever come back. I was thinking things like that when Nanna told me to carry Tomas, which helped take my thoughts off J.W., a little anyway.

Heavy, dark clouds blowing in looking like I feel, and Poppa said he can smell rain. End. TAV

I almost forgot. Mr. Bulleau does not think the Indians that have been following us are Sioux. End again. TAV

Friday morning the 8th

Dear Aria,

An emergency meeting is taking place near Mr. Keil's coach. 3 cattle and 2 horses are missing and were probably stolen from the herd during last night's storm. Everyone suspects the Indians who have been following us, and a number of people want to go after them. Mr.

Bulleau said no, we have no proof anything was stolen and, besides, someone would probably shoot themselves by mistake. Mr. Hesse thought they might come back if we let them get away with stealing so easily. Mr. Bulleau didn't think so, but a lot of people disagreed with him, and then someone reminded the group about the Hesse girls and that we had to teach the Indians a lesson. Mr. Bulleau got very angry, but no one was listening to him, so he called us all fool amateurs and stomped off. Mr. Keil raised his arms and called for order and it took him several minutes to calm everyone down. He was for listening to Mr. Bulleau — and most people agreed — but some still wanted to look for the thieves. The meeting broke up into little groups, and I saw J.W. with his father and several other men and women. Mary Margaret said she had to help her mother, and I decided to go back to the wagon. Nanna was following Tomas as he waddled thru the grass and underneath the Empress Christina. Momma was baking bread. Everything looked so normal, you would not guess that such an angry meeting was going on at the same time. End. TAV

Later: 8 men have gone off after the thieves, including Mr. Hesse. Mr. Bulleau warned them not to do anything stupid. He also said he was not waiting for them and ordered us to get ready to leave. Volunteers will drive their wagons if needed. I heard Poppa tell Momma and Nanna that there are very bad feelings about Mr. Bulleau and the Indians, but that he agreed about not going after the thieves. What if all the Indians come back? he wanted to know. Ernesto said he wasn't afraid of any number of Indians and wished he could go with the posse and shoot them, and Poppa said he was being silly even for a 10-year-old and did not understand what he was saying. Ernesto said he did too and that Poppa was just scared. Nanna was shocked when she heard this and told him to hold his tongue or he would feel the cane on his backside. Momma would never allow that, so Ernesto did not hold his tongue — until Poppa told him if he was going to act like a baby he could stay with Tomas all day. And Momma agreed. It promises to be a hot day. End. TAV

Friday, June 8, 1883

Dear Aria,

Ernesto has to stay in the wagon today for talking back, and the Empress Christina and General O'Brien are both clomping along behind. Mr. Cross let me ride with him in the morning. I asked how the cattle and horses could have been stolen, since we had guards watching them. He thought the thieves wore dark buffalo skins so they could creep close during the downpour. Then they gently separated a few animals from the herd and "absquatulated with their booty." The story was nice, but I liked the big word best. I asked what it meant and had Mr. Cross say it and spell it several times. Up until now, the biggest work I knew was Mississippi. Teresa wants you back.

Good-night friend, Antoinetta

Still Friday the 8th

Dear Aria,

No sign of the men, so Mr. Bulleau sent someone out to see if they were all right. We are almost off Indian land, which is a great relief to Momma. Am going to visit Mary Margaret now. Have not seen J.W. since the meeting. End. TAV

Saturday the 9th

Dear Aria,

The men have returned and all are safe. They seemed pleased with themselves and each other, even tho they only got 2 steers back — the other being shot by accident by 1 of our men. The Indians rode away with the horses, and our men decided it was too dark to follow. 1 of our men bragged about the fight, and Mr. Bulleau told him he read too many dime novels for his own good. That started another big argument, and Mr. Keil and Mr. Anderson had to pull the 2 apart, with Mr. Keil saying, "Friends, friends, remember the spirit of our adventure. There is no need for uncivil words," to which Mr. Bulleau said, "Words! I'll let him feel an uncivil fist, I will!" When Momma heard about the fight she said that Netta and I could not go to any more meetings. Netta was upset and said it wasn't fair, but I didn't. Since leaving Watertown Momma has issued many "do nots" and forgotten just about all of them. Maybe she is distracted or maybe she is tired — all I know is that Momma lets me do things she would not back on Wooster Street. She even told me I drive the wagon better than Poppa, but that I shouldn't tell him she said so. J.W. rode past our wagon today and did not say hello or even tip his hat to Momma! At first I felt hurt and blamed myself and my bad temper. Now I think he is just being a stupid little boy and rude besides. I do not like wasting all these thoughts on someone so stubborn. Hot, dry, and little wind today. Could see dark shapes far off to the southwest, which Shep thinks might be the Black Hills. End. TAV

Still Saturday

Dear Aria,

Mary Margaret was helping cook supper when her dress caught fire and blazed up!! Luckily, her mother pushed her to the ground and beat out the flames, but not before Mary Margaret's legs and arms were burned. I visited awhile and read her some of JOHN HALIFAX, GENTLEMAN, and we laughed a little like before. Her legs hurt, but she is most upset because her long hair was singed and had to be cut off short. I am going over there now to see if her mother needs any help. End. TAV

Sunday the 10th

Dear Aria,

Mary Margaret's legs did not hurt as much today, but the henbane made her tired, and she slept a lot even with her wagon bumping along. I went back and forth between their wagon and ours to help her mother, who is still upset and nervous about what happened. She seems happy to have someone to talk to when Mary Margaret is asleep. Her husband hardly talks, tho he is a kind man and treats his horses gently. I am almost as tired as after the first day's walking, but the work and talk have kept my mind clear of *him*. To sleep. End. TAV

Monday the 11th

Dear Aria,

All done in — and I still have to clean dishes and the kettle, then go over to see Mary Margaret and help her mother. I was able to rest when the train encountered a herd of cattle heading north for summer grazing. The cattle trail runs from down near Mexico all the way up north near Canada, and is some 400 yards wide and worn deep like a dry riverbed. It took nearly an hour for the cattle to pass, and I fell asleep with Tomas in the wagon. Nanna said *he* rode by our wagon more than once, and said hello to her each time. I wonder what that means — if anything. End. TAV

Monday, June 11, 1883

Dear Aria,

Edi and I talked with a real cowboy today. He had ridden away from the herd to get a calf when he saw us. He said hello, and we said it was nice to meet him and asked where he was from. He said, "Oh, here and thare, and sumtimes in-b'tween, but mostly wharever thare's food'n a fire'n work." We gave him a yellow flower that he stuck in the band of his hat, then he tipped it in our direction, and rode off with the calf over his saddle.

Sincerely, Antoinetta

Tuesday the 12th

Dear Aria,

Rode with Mary Margaret most of the day. She is feeling better — and much hungrier! I had to run back to our wagon twice for the biscuits Momma had made in the morning, and Nanna smiled and said our family had been blessed with another hungry girl. Netta said *he* stopped her and asked if I was okay, but when she told him where I was he rode off scowling. Netta wanted to know why he was annoyed and why I had such a strange look on my face, and I told her to mind her own business, which wasn't very nice, I suppose. I guess Netta has not read my part of the diary since I told her not to, so I shouldn't be upset if she is curious. End. TAV

Wednesday the 13th

Dear Aria,

Mary Margaret much better and we had a fine ride today. The train came upon a tiny, window-less cabin — if you can call a pile of sticks, broken boards, pieces of wood, animal hides, and grass a cabin! — next to a small, clear pond. An ancient-looking man hobbled out of the cabin. He had a long, scraggly beard, unwashed hair down his back, and very few teeth in his head that I could see. As soon as she saw him, Nanna made the sign of the cross and whispered, "It is Saint Onofrius reborn!" The man seemed troubled by the light, but managed to look all along the train, then said he would sell us water for $5 a wagon. Mr. Bulleau said we don't pay for water on open grasslands, and the man said he owned the land and water, and Mr. Bulleau said prove it. Back and forth, back and forth, they went until it was decided that $5 would pay for *all* of the wagons and stock. The old man called us thieves, but he pocketed the coins and went back inside his cabin. From inside, he kept on complaining the entire time we got water and probably when the stock was watering as well. Mr. Bulleau said the man has lived there for over 10 years and tries to charge anyone who happens by for water — lone travelers, cattle herds, army soldiers, priests and preachers, even Indians. Mr. Bulleau has no idea what he does with his money, or even what his name is. Mary Margaret and I talked about J.W. — yes, I have decided to use his initials again — and she said I was right to be annoyed at him and that boys can be stupid. She also said I shouldn't be stupid and just stew about him, I should say something to him and be done with it. I am not sure I can do this, but I did practice what I might say and how I would say it. End. TAV

Wednesday, June 13, 1883

Dear Aria,

Edi and I were playing when I slipped and sat down in the pond. It was great fun, until I thought of Momma and what she would say. But she did not say anything, except that I should change, wash my dress and stockings, and clean my shoes. I think Momma's back must be hurting again for her to say nothing. Nanna did say something, so I guess her back does not hurt.

Yours wet and dry, Antoinetta

Friday the 15th

Dear Aria,

Crossed another cattle route, tho we saw nothing of the cattle except their chips. Made good time even in the hot weather, and came upon 4 wagons near a stream late in the day. A sign on 1 of the wagons said HYPOLITE LA BRIE'S TRAVELLING VARIETY SHOW: SHAKESPEER OUR SPECIALTY. Mr. Bulleau wanted to continue, but Mr. Keil and the Association persuaded him to stop for the night so straggling wagons could catch up. Mr. Keil asked Mr. La Brie to perform for the train — I think to get our minds off all the bad that has happened and all of the angry words — but Mr. La Brie said no. He held up a copy of the *Black Hills Pioneer* newspaper with a headline that read: SILVER FOUND! All his players — except for 1 boy — had left for the diggings in the Black Hills, and took all his horses besides.

People from the train crowded around Mr. La Brie to ask him where the silver mines were located, and Mr. La Brie read parts of the article out-loud, which made everyone even more excited. Mr. Keil looked worried and I think he was sorry he made Mr. Bulleau stop the train. Everyone was talking now — Uncle Eugenio and Poppa included — and went on talking. Momma pushed into the crowd — and she has never *ever* done anything like that before! — to get Poppa to move the wagon and take care of Zephaniah and Red Top. But half the train just sat where it had stopped for an hour or longer — horses and oxen still hitched up, pawing the ground, snorting, and waiting — while men and women and children chattered on about silver. End. TAV

9 o'clock: Poppa said I can use the fire for 5 minutes more only. Mr. Keil and the rest of the Association went thru camp earlier, trying to calm people about the silver strike. They said the reports might be false, that the land might be privately owned, that there might not be very much silver. "Remember, you're a part of a community now, a very special 1 where you'll have a fair chance to succeed, to prove yourself," Mr. Keil pleaded. "Don't throw it away because of a newspaper story." Uncle Eugenio told them that having a silver strike so close was also an opportunity and then asked, "And aren't you a little curious about the silver too? A little bit?" Mr. Keil hesitated a second, then said, "A little, yes. I admit it. I am a little curious. But not enough to take me away from our adventure here." But that tiny bit of delay before answering the question told me he was more than just a little curious. And it said the same thing to a lot of other people too. "Think about what you have right here, in this community," Mr. Keil said, and many people nodded their heads in agreement, but not everyone. "But think about what might be out there in the silver fields just waiting for us to take it," the tall man with the stern look answered. "Think about that too." And many people nodded their heads to his words. All of this talk made me nervous — because it was just like the talk that got us here in the first place. Time to put out the fire, says Poppa. End. TAV

Saturday, June 16, 1883

Dear Aria,

Last night after supper, I went to tell Mr. La Brie that Shakespeare was misspelled. I could not find Mr. La Brie, but a boy named William was there. I told him, but he told me Mr.

La Brie didn't care anymore. The Association had agreed to sell him two horses, and Mr. La Brie and the boy were leaving for the silver fields in the morning. And it is true; they left before the sun came up today. William also said that Hypolite La Brie was a made-up name. Mr. La Brie's real name is Walter Cooper and he's from Kansas. William showed me the inside of the costume wagon and let me try on a red wig and sword. Mr. La Brie came back then, but did not mind that we were playing. He even said I could take anything I wanted, so I took the red wig and sword. Mr. La Brie gave me his copy of the Black Hills Pioneer *too, so I would remember I was a part of history. Poppa laughed out loud when he saw me. Momma said I looked ridiculous, but she smiled also. Nanna has found some wild onions and greens and says she will make us soup for supper. I am hungry already!*

Sincerely, Antoinetta

SILVER FOUND!

RICH VEIN OPENED IN BLACK HILLS REGION
A BELT OF SILVER 20 MILES WIDE
ARMY TO MAINTAIN ORDER
THE LAND OF PROMISE!

Yesterday, by way of telegraph, we learned that a rich vein of high-grade silver had been found in the mountains surrounding Pringle. The strike was made over two weeks ago, and a claim filed at the United States Assay Office in Hot Springs. It is reported that the Chief of Assay Operations, Justin Longford Bigelow, will travel to the claim in order to inspect and verify it. There is speculation that, judging by the type and formation of the rocks in the region, the vein could be from ten to twenty miles wide and ten miles long. "Quite possibly," an informant in Hot Springs tells us, "this may be as rich a strike as in the history of the Black Hills." Already, the roads leading to the area are growing crowded with would-be fortune seekers, and one hundred or more individuals have already filed claims of their own. No reports of violence have been made, but town officials warn that supervision by the United States Army will be requested, and that all crimes, major and minor, will be prosecuted to their full term. One employee of this newspaper has already resigned to join in the search for silver. Before leaving he said: "I am going to dig my fortune out of the rocks with my own hands. I am going to the Land of Promise!" This newspaper is sending special correspondent William Stone to the area, and his detailed reports will appear in daily form.

Saturday the 16th

Dear Aria,

What a queer day this has been. We began the morning by learning that Mr. La Brie and the boy had left for the silver mines. As usual, we had breakfast and then packed the wagon, but very few others did and the train did not leave. Mr. Bulleau was furious and shouted at everybody to get ready, but this time, some men told Mr. Bulleau to be quiet and that he was just a hired hand! Mr. Keil and Mr. Anderson spent a lot of time with Mr. Bulleau, trying to calm him down, but I think it would take an army of Mrs. Currans to do that. Finally, Mr. Bulleau went off to help with the stock, saying we could stay a day and then he and his men were leaving. Men and women were gathered everywhere in little circles, talking, talking, talking, sometimes loudly. Poppa, Uncle Eugenio, and the other men from our street were at the Grosso's wagon and they all looked so serious. Momma tried to keep busy, but she was worried and kept glancing at the men. Nanna sniffed and said they looked like "gentry making big decisions that we will have to clean up." When Mrs. Grosso brought coffee to the group, the men stopped talking until she left them. And when Netta went over wearing her red wig and sword, Poppa barked at her to stop playing near them.

At 1 point, Poppa came over and told Momma that Uncle Eugenio wanted to look for silver, and that the others did too. Uncle Eugenio said we had to act quickly, before everyone in the country came running. That was what he had said about Idaho, Momma reminded him. "I know, I know," Poppa said, "and I told him so. I did, I said, 'Eugenio, everything we have is in those wagons and the land in Idaho.' I told him, 'We cannot afford to lose any of it.' I told him that. But you know Eugenio and his ways. He can be persuasive. And the others agree with him." Momma told him it was foolish to go off. Her voice was only a little louder than usual, but I could tell she was furious at Uncle Eugenio *and* Poppa. And so was I. When has he ever dug for anything besides onions! Momma wanted to know. They talked some more, but I couldn't hear much except when Poppa said, "But he is my older brother." I could hear it in Poppa's voice and so could Momma — we had been forced to leave Wooster Street and everything and everyone we knew because of Uncle Eugenio, and now it was going to happen again. What about having a fair chance in Opportunity and working hard and making a better life for us, I wanted to ask him. Or was that just talk? I must have looked very upset because Nanna told me not to worry and sent me to get water, which I was happy to do.

I went to Mary Margaret's first, and she said she wanted to walk a little, so she came with me to the stream. She said her father wanted to look for silver too, but her mother told him she wasn't going with him and that if he left he shouldn't bother coming back. I was shocked that she would say this, but Mary Margaret swore that's what happened, and her grandparents agreed with her mother — and they are her father's parents! I wish Momma could be so bold, but I do not think she would ever talk to Poppa like that. She says what she thinks, but softly so she does not embarrass or show disrespect to Poppa in front of others. That was when I saw Ernesto and a group of the other children. Ernesto had on a metal helmet like those worn by Roman soldiers, tho his was much dented, while others were wearing long caps, hats with big orange feathers, odd-looking dresses and baggy pants, and all sorts of wigs. Some carried swords and shields. Mr. La Brie had left the door to his costume wagon open with a note saying we could take anything we wanted. And that is how the day went — people talking and arguing and planning, children running through camp in silly costumes play-acting. Mr. Keil looking upset and more and more tired, but still saying, "Remember your dreams, friends, remember the opportunities that await us," tho fewer and fewer people were listening to him by this time. End. TAV

8 o'clock: There was another meeting just after supper. I think Mr. Keil knows that for many the idea of silver is stronger than the idea of Idaho because he did not spend much time trying to change people's minds. He said that anyone who wanted to could go to the silver diggings and no hard feelings, that everyone owned their own wagons and animals. He added that the train would leave in the morning and then urged that even if a man wanted to look for silver, he should allow his family to go on. Their families would be safer with the train, he pointed out, and if the silver fields weren't everything they expected, they could turn around and follow us easily. Mr. Bulleau had agreed to do a map to show them what our route would be and how to find us.

That seemed to quiet some of the hard feelings and worries. The men could ride off on their foolish little adventure, and when they have learned their lesson they can come back to the wagons and their families. That's how Momma put it anyway. And that's what Uncle Eugenio and Poppa and the others from our street — except for Mr. Cardi — decided to do. I was glad too. I had heard enough about Idaho and our future community to picture it, but a mining camp sounded like a wild place if it needed the United States Army to stop all crimes, major and minor.

Mr. Cardi said he would stay and watch over the other men's families and possessions. Poppa said I would drive the wagon and Ernesto would help tend the stock herd. Ernesto did not like that I was driving, but Momma told him to shush and do as he was told. The only other time I remember Momma looking so sad was during the weeks before we left Wooster Street. Nanna had been happy to leave Wooster Street, but she was not happy about Uncle Eugenio and Poppa leaving now. "They are like donkeys in a line. Each one thinks he is following something sweet, but he is really just following another smelly donkey." End. TAV

Monday the 18th

Dear Aria,

2 long days and hot besides. They — 27 men, 4 with their families — rode off early Saturday morning with much cheerful shouting and waving and promises to come back rich. Poppa gave us all a hug and many kisses, and whispered to me to take care of Momma and not to let Nanna bother me too much. Momma was quiet and I

could tell that she had cried during the night. Nanna did not say anything about men being foolish — she just shook her head and looked angry. We watched them ride across the grass until Mr. Bulleau rode up and down the train telling us to get ready to leave. Since Shep went off too, Mr. Cardi helped me yoke Zephaniah and Red Top, and then our day's journey began — tho much more quietly than the men's. The only unusual thing was that Aunt Marta pulled in directly behind us and Rosaria actually smiled at me.

Travel very slow because so many like Aunt Marta are new to driving and there are so few men to help ease wagons down or push them up steep hills. But we made 10 miles. At 1 dry riverbed, J.W. helped push us. I wanted to say something to him — and almost did — but there was so much activity that I had to drive off before I could get his attention. He is now with the herd for the night. Not enough water in the barrel to wash off the dust, which has settled in every part of my body and clothes. Besides, I am too tired and so I will End for now. TAV

Tuesday, June 19, 1883

Dear Aria,

We were riding with Mr. Cross when little Charlie fell. He was inside his wagon one moment, on the ground holding his

arm and crying the next. Mr. Cross stopped his team, and we all ran to see how badly Charlie was hurt. His arm is broken, but he stopped crying after Mr. Bulleau and Mr. Keil had a splint on it (the one person trained in medicine having gone off to look for silver). I noticed that Mr. Cross had trouble climbing back up onto his wagon. He said his head hurt and his stomach was sour, but that someone near the very front of the train felt even worse, so he wasn't complaining. I told him about the medicine the Irish Brigade had sent over for Momma. He said that potion would cure many ills, but not his stomach. He did not tell us any long stories, which was unusual. Edi said he would tell us a story when he felt better.
Sincerely, Antoinetta

Wednesday the 20th

Dear Aria,

Several in the train are ill, and we have 1 broken arm as well, but we still had few delays and made 12 miles. End. TAV

9 o'clock: Aunt Marta and Mrs. Grosso had a loud argument tonight, and Nanna and Momma went over to help settle matters. While they were talking, Rosaria came over and asked me how to pronounce several words from her book on geography, which I did as best as I could. She said thank you — which is something she never said to me before! — and then asked if she could ask me questions about geography when she had them. I said yes, and thought that this journey has certainly changed us all in many ways. From where I am writing this, I can see the Anderson wagon and the shadows of people moving around their fire, but I do not think I will go over. Usually, I do and say things without thinking, and get myself into trouble. Now I am thinking and thinking but not doing anything — and feeling bad anyway. I am not sure which 1 is worse. End. TAV

Thursday the 21st

Dear Aria,

Some of the sick are feeling a little better, some are worse. 3 of Mr. Bulleau's men are ill, and several others in the train besides. The illness seems particularly hard on the few men left. Slow going in the morning and the train broke in 2. The lead wagons went a mile ahead of the rest. We could have stayed with the lead — Zephaniah and Red Top have never missed a step — but Mrs. Grosso was having trouble driving, and Mr. Cardi thought we should stay together. The Anderson wagon was with the lead group, and I worried all afternoon that it might be days before we catch up with them — which is why I did what I did when we caught up with them later. I went — no, I marched right over to the Andersons' wagon determined to have my talk. J.W. said he was exhausted and did not feel well — and he did look all done in — but I said I needed to say something and he needed to listen. When I asked if he had been staying away from me because he was angry, he said he thought *I* was the 1 who was angry and that *I* was staying away from him. I was about to say that was silly when I remembered how that word had made me so upset the last time and decided not to use it. So I said I was never angry, not enough to stay away from him, and he said he was never really that angry either. I said I wanted both him and Mary Margaret to be my friends, and he said that was fine with him. I should have been happy with that, I guess, but I decided I never wanted to feel so bad again, and I told J.W. that he had to promise to talk with me if we ever have a problem and not go around with the bad feelings inside. I wasn't sure what to say after this and J.W. seemed to be waiting for me to start. So I asked him what he had been doing since the men had gone off. We talked a little after this, but I felt shy and I think he did too. But at least we talked — and now Mary Margaret will not give me any more disapproving looks. End. TAV

Friday the 22nd

Dear Aria,

Woke to discover that Cora Schlissel — a baby 3 months of age — had died in the night of the fever, with her mother severely sick too. Much care was taken with the child's burial and Mr. Bulleau did not even seem restless to be moving. I heard him tell Mr. Keil that another of his men is ill, which makes 4. There is no 1 to drive Mrs. Schlissel's wagon, so she will have to stay until she is better. Another woman and her husband and their 3 children will stay to take care of her. Mr. Keil did not want to leave them, but Mr. Bulleau said it will be 2 or 3 days til we come to good water. So we left the 2 wagons and the little grave behind with heavy hearts. End. TAV

7 o'clock: Mary Margaret visited and then J.W. I was nervous at first, but everyone was very civil, which is a start, I think. J.W. says Mr. Bulleau thinks the sickness is Spanish fever and that we got it from the cattle herd we met days ago. Aunt Marta blames the Indians, Mr. Cardi blames Mr. La Brie and the boy William, while Momma thinks it's the heat and water. Nanna said it was none of those things and pointed to the black wagon carrying Willie Keil. End. TAV

Saturday the 23rd

Dear Aria,

1 of Mr. Bulleau's men died — and he had not even been sick yesterday! Mr. Keil's sister is very ill, and so is 1 of Mr. Keil's drivers. The train split up again, with 8 wagons trailing. We were able to keep up, but even Zephaniah and Red Top struggled whenever the land angled up. Their ribs are showing very clearly, as if they were drying up for lack of water. End. TAV

Saturday, June 23, 1883

Dear Aria,

I have had a queer stomach — maybe from one of Teresa's suppers, but I would never say that to her — for two days and did not feel like writing. My stomach feels a little better today, so I will write. Edi's father is sick, so Edi must care for him, while her mother is driving. Mr. Cross is better, but Coyote Cal is not, but I could not visit them. Momma is worried about the fever and said I must stay close to our wagon. I did not tell her about my stomach or she would not have let me out of the wagon at all. I did ride next to Teresa today, and she showed me how to hold the reins and what to say. Zephaniah looked around at me and snorted whenever I gave him a command, and I am not sure I liked

the way he snorted. I think he is an animal with too many
opinions.

Sincerely, Antoinetta

Later Saturday: Went to Mary Margaret's and everyone was well. When I got back to our wagon, I found J.W. waiting. Mr. Bulleau is sending someone out after the men with word to meet us at the next water. J.W. is still tired-looking and covered with dust and grime, but he seemed less shy. Mr. Cardi said we should lighten the wagons if we want to keep up tomorrow. Momma did not argue, and took several boxes from the wagon and left them in the grass. All of our things in Uncle Eugenio's wagon were also left, so I can finally say good-bye to my Sunday dresses. End. TAV

Sunday the 24th

Dear Aria,

Began the day by burying Willie Keil, to free up that wagon to carry the sick. There were not many people there, not like when Hildi and Caterina were buried, and Mr. Keil did not talk very much. He apologized to Willie for not being able to keep his promise about bringing him to Opportunity, but said he would try to come back for him soon. "We may be leaving you here, but your spirit will travel with us always." Then in a shaky voice, he led the group in a sweet hymn. Mary Margaret showed me the words in her PRAISE BOOK and I will copy them down to remember how sad Mr. Keil was:

Around the Throne of God in heaven
    Thousands of children stand;
Children whose sins are all forgiven,
    A holy, happy band.
In flowing robes of spotless white
    See every one arrayed;
Dwelling in everlasting light,
And joys that never fade.

We left a little after this and we were such quiet travelers that every so often I could hear Mr. Keil's voice come floating back singing the hymn over and over again.

Water very low, but Mr. Cardi says that if we conserve what we have we can make it to the next water. Aunt Marta does not look well, and my cousin Rosaria is not feeling well either, but my aunt says she can drive and will keep up. We will see. End. TAV

Monday the 25th

Dear Aria,

We have been left behind — our wagon and Aunt Marta's. Yesterday, Aunt Marta did not feel well after lunch, but managed to drive her wagon til the train stopped for the night. She grew worse during the night, as did Rosaria. Ernesto also does not feel well and Momma worries that they all have the fever. Mr. Cardi wanted everyone from our street to stay together, but Momma said it was dangerous for the others, especially the children. There was some talk about Netta and I going with them, but we both said no and that was that. They gave us as much water as they could spare, and Mr. Cardi said he would return as soon as they could get more. Mr. Keil apologized that there was not an extra man to leave behind, and drew a map showing the route they would be following as well as some of the trails Mr. Bulleau knew about up ahead. He also told Momma that he would be happy to carry her piano for as long as he could, and Momma said that was very kind. Then the train left. Mary Margaret cried when I told her, and hugged me, and J.W. said he would be back for me — and kissed me even tho Momma and Nanna were right there.

Our wagons and tents sit on a hill with a far view of the Black Hills and waves and waves of nothing in-between. The last wagon disappeared from sight just before 11 o'clock. The only sign that they ever existed are the wheel tracks thru the grass. This is a very big land, and our wagons seem tiny indeed sitting in the middle of it. End. TAV

Monday, June 25, 1883

Dear Aria,

Aunt Marta was very sick during the night, and suffered much from the bowel complaint. Momma told us it might be a few days before everyone is better. As the train went past, everyone looked sad and wished us good luck and said they would be waiting for us up ahead. Edi said don't get lost and waved so much, I thought her arm would drop right off. Mr. Cross, who is feeling a little better and can drive himself, said to take care and that he would remember us in his prayers. I told him I could remember him without my prayers, and he laughed out loud. I am going to help Momma take care of Aunt Marta and Cousin Rosaria so they can get better fast and I can be with my friends again.
Sincerely, Antoinetta

Still Monday

Momma and Nanna very busy with the sick today. Momma had me air out the wagon and clean it. Hunted for edible plants in the afternoon and was foolish enough to get lost. I was very upset and disorganized until I remembered that the Black Hills had been directly behind me when I set out, so I walked directly toward them and soon saw our wagons. Sun was melting hot all day, but the night is chilly. I wonder where Poppa and the others are right now, and what Mary Margaret and J.W. are doing? End. TAV

Tuesday the 26th

Dear Aria,

Ernesto was up most of the night in great pain. When I brought in water, he was sweating and restless and did not recognize me. Aunt Marta is much the same as yesterday, but Rosaria seems better, tho very weak, and said I was kind and that she hoped I would forgive her for being so mean in the past. I said I did and even held her hand for a while to show that I meant it. I am worried about Momma. At breakfast she sat staring at the fire and hardly touched her food. Nanna said she will be fine, but I am not so sure. Tomas walked around camp several times and never seemed bothered by the heat or tall grass. End. TAV

In the afternoon: 2 of the trailing wagons came past. No 1 got down from their wagons to visit, but they did stop long enough to say that Mrs. Schlissel had died, and that many others are sick. After the wagons had gone, I saw Momma looking in the direction of Rapid City. She was probably thinking of Poppa, and I was too. Where is he? End. TAV

8 o'clock: We are going to Rapid City! Not the wagons, just Nanna and me. Ernesto is worse and Momma wants us to find Poppa and Uncle Eugenio and get them to come back here fast. Nanna said she would drag them back by their ears if they said no, and I believe she could. I did not want to go, but Momma said Nanna could not manage the trip herself and that Netta could not handle General O'Brien or the trail. I am not sure I can either, but Momma said I could. I would have protested more, but Momma looked so tired that I said I would do my best. And so we will set out tomorrow at sunrise. End. TAV

Tuesday, June 26, 1883

Dear Aria,

Teresa said I could have you for the night, but that she is taking you with her. I do not think this is fair or wise. You

would be much safer here than out there where you could get lost. I thought about hiding you, but I am sure Momma would take Teresa's part, so I don't think that plan would work. I have ripped pages from the back, however, and they will have to do while you are out traveling. Edi could think of a better plan, but this is the best I can do. There is nothing else to write.

Sincerely, Antoinetta

Wednesday: I don't have time to write very much, so I think Netta will forgive me if I don't write the date and so on. We have stopped to rest after traveling most of the morning, me walking and leading General O'Brien with Nanna on him — along with our water, a satchel of food, the rifle, a small cooking kettle, and blankets. Felt as if we went downhill for an hour, then up and over 1 grassy wave after another. We could see the wagon for several hours — with Netta waving and waving and me waving back — then we went up and over 1 more incline and it was gone. It was as if the wagon and everyone had been eaten up by the land. Nanna just said we must go before her bones refuse to move, so I must end here.

Later: We have no watch, so we do not know what time it is. We don't even know how far we've gone. The sun is in the right place — to our right — so I think we're going the way we should. Nanna decided to walk after our stop and when I said the walking would be hard she said, "I'm an old woman, but don't treat me like 1," so I won't. General O'Brien looks happier too. We are still looking for the trail to Rapid C — Nanna just spotted a rider a mile or so away and said we should not move or let him see us. So we will sit until he has gone. I took out the rifle and put in bullets just as I had seen Poppa do, held it up to my shoulder as if I was going to shoot, but kept my finger clear of the trigger. Nanna told me to stop playing and put the rifle down. I am not eager to shoot it, but thought I should hold it once just so I know what it feels like. We are off again.

Dusk: We have stopped for the night because Nanna is afraid we might miss the trail in the dark and walk miles and miles out of our way. I made a fire of grass and sticks, bits of wood and a pile of dry bones — which might be from a buffalo or a steer, but without the skull it is hard for me to tell which. Nanna is trying to toast pieces of bread and worrying that the fire is too big. She is afraid some Indians might see it and come for us. I am worried that coyotes — who are calling to each other right now — might come for a visit and I want the fire as big as possible to scare them off. My fingers are feeling stiff from the cold so I am going to stop writing and roll myself up in my blanket. I hope that Ernesto and Aunt Marta and Cousin Rosaria are better and that Poppa is the 1 who sees our fire and finds us. End.

Thursday: A new day and the dark shape of the mountains doesn't look any closer than yesterday morning. I found a tiny stream not far from our camp and filled our cask with fresh water. Nanna said that on her trip from Italy to New York, clean, cool water was the thing she missed most. She took a long drink and pronounced it as sweet as Baby Tomas's smile. We are off.

Later: Not 100 long steps from our camp was the trail — 2 wagon wheel tracks deeply cutting thru the thick grass down to bare dirt and running north and south. At least we hope it is the trail. To the north is where Mary Margaret and J.W. are waiting with the rest of those going to Opportunity. To the south is Rapid City and Poppa — I hope. We walked along — me in 1 track, Nanna in the other because it is easier walking there than through the grass growing between — with General O'Brien trailing behind on a long lead. Found myself thinking some bad things I did not want to think — and won't even write here! — so I said prayers for Ernesto, Aunt Marta, Rosaria, then recited the capitals of the states — the ones I knew — and thought about all of the things we have not had to eat since we left New York — oranges, figs, goat cheese, and crusty dark bread, a thick *astrato* with *capelli d'àngelo* and meatballs, and sugar-coated almonds. Next I tried to remember being with Francesca, and how we talked and talked about everything, but I couldn't recall how her voice sounded. I could see her and her smile, and the way her eyes could sparkle when she was excited. And I could even remember a lot of what she said. But I just couldn't hear her talking! This was almost as upsetting as the bad thoughts I was having, and the only thing I could think to do was sing a song out loud I'd heard 1 Sunday in camp:

> *Star of peace to wanderers weary!*
> *Bright the beams that smile on me;*
> *Cheer this pilot's vision dreary,*
> *Far, far at sea.*
> *Star Divine! Oh, safely guide me,*
> *Bring this wanderer home to thee;*
> *Sore temptations long have tried me,*
> *Far, far at sea.*

I could feel Nanna staring at me, but she didn't say anything. I was happy about that because singing the words over and over made me feel peaceful and helped me ignore the way my feet hurt. End.

Noon or so: We have stopped to eat at a spot where another trail runs off the main 1 at a right angle. It seems to head directly to the Black Hills, but doesn't look well used, and I think we should stay on the main trail even if it does not seem so direct. Nanna worries that the men went on this other trail, but I don't think they would because I saw the map Mr. Bulleau gave the men and it did not have any trails but the main 1 on it. Nanna said we will follow my trail. When did it become *my* trail?

In the afternoon: We have come across a mailbox set up at the side of the trail where another trail shoots off in both directions. I peeked inside — and there was a real letter in it, stamps and all. The letter was going to "Mr. Prescott Wayne, San Francisco." Nanna did not think it would ever find Mr. Prescott Wayne, but I do. And if I had envelopes and stamps, I would send letters to my friends from here too.

Later still: It is very late at night — after 10 I would guess — and Nanna is asleep. I can't close my eyes and don't know whether to laugh or cry since I have been doing a little of both all night and here is why. Late in the afternoon, Nanna's feet began to hurt and General O'Brien suddenly got balky, so we decided that was as good a place as any to stay the night. Nanna was off gathering sticks and grass for a fire, and I was unpacking General O'Brien when 2 men came riding over a hill and saw us. I didn't even see them approaching. They were just there, right next to Nanna in an instant and I think both Nanna and I were surprised and a little scared.

They were rough-looking, tho no rougher-looking than Mr. Bulleau's men, but they had a way of looking at us and our things that bothered me. Nanna asked them in Italian what they wanted, but they had no idea what she said, so they asked me if I spoke American. I told them what Nanna said and they both smiled, all the while looking around as if searching for someone. 1 got off his horse and said, "Seems like yer pretty much alone, here, doesn't it?" It was plain that Nanna did not like these 2 because she told them we were busy and to leave, but they didn't bother with Nanna anymore. The second man dismounted and told me that they were going to the silver fields and could use our mule and our supplies and they would give me $5 for them. Nanna understood enough to say no, and I said no too and told told them we needed our things to get to Rapid City, but the first man said where they were going was more important and we should take the $5. Nanna said no again and ordered the 2 to leave and called them *banditi*, which annoyed the first man enough that he told Nanna to shut up — which Nanna did not do. The other took out a coin and said they didn't want to talk anymore, the deal was settled and here was the money, but Nanna hit his hand and sent the coin sailing into the grass. Both men were yelling at Nanna now, and she was between them, turning to scold 1 and then the other, which is when I took out the rifle and pointed it at them. "Leave Nanna alone!" I screamed, which got everyone's attention, so I screamed again, "Leave her alone and get out of here!" The first man said I was being silly, while his friend said, "Put that damd rifle down or else," and even Nanna wanted to know what I thought I was doing! But I held the rifle as steady as I could and told the men to leave or they would be sorry. "Damd crazy girl," the 1 who'd lost the $5 yelled, "give me that thing bafor ya shoot yer-self" and he took a step toward me — which was the wrong thing to do because it scared me enough that my finger twitched on the trigger. I had pointed the rifle at the men to scare them, and had forgotten that it was loaded from the day before, so when my finger hit the trigger, I was as surprised as anybody when the rifle went off with a roar and blast of white smoke. The rifle jumped in my hands, hit me in the chin, and knocked me to the ground, but I was alert enough to pick it up and cock it again and level it at the man while in a sitting position. "Hold on there, missy," the man said, but he wasn't yelling anymore. He took a big step backwards, his eyes real wide. I think the bullet must have sailed close by his head because he was touching his ear to see if it was still there. Nanna's mouth hung open a second, then she started yelling that good girls don't shoot at people, and that they especially don't shoot their own Nanna, which would be a terrible sin and put me in hell with all sorts of bad people. The other man looked so mad it was scary and he started to take a pistol from his holster. "I've had 'nough this — !" he shouted, but before he had his gun pointed at me, I pulled the trigger again. This time I held on tighter and the rifle didn't knock me over when it went off, but just rocked me back a little. I cocked it again and swung the rifle back and forth between the 2 men. Every time the rifle pointed toward the first man, he ducked a little and took another step back. Meanwhile, the second man — who had dropped his pistol — bent down to pick it up, so I told him leave it and when he talked back I pulled the trigger a third time, this time blasting up a chunk of dirt right near his hand, tho I was sure I had aimed it over his head. Nanna was still yelling at me, the first man was saying I was too crazy to reason with and that he and his friend should leave, while his friend called me a string of cuss words that would have impressed any of Mr. Bulleau's men. But he didn't reach down for his pistol again. Instead he and his friend retreated to their horses very quickly. The really angry man said he would come back to get me, and I almost pulled the trigger again, but I noticed that as he said this he had turned his horse and was hurrying off. Which left me holding the rifle pointed in the general direction of Nanna, who was still saying things to me, tho not quite as loudly as before. I was glad I was sitting down, because I suddenly felt lightheaded, but I didn't want to be sick as long as those men were in sight, so all I could think to do was yell at Nanna to shut up. And she did! Nanna scowled at me, then turned back to gathering wood. I took a deep breath and stood up. My legs were wobbly, but I thought I should watch to make sure the men rode off and didn't circle back to get us. It was very quiet after this and the acrid smell of gun smoke tickled my nose, but I never took my eyes off the men til they were gone from sight. That's when I turned and told Nanna I was sorry for pointing the rifle at her and scaring her, but that I didn't know what else to do, and that I didn't mean to yell at her either. I thought she was going to scold me again, but instead she said, "You were like 1 of Garibaldi's warriors, Teresa! You gave those 2 bandits what they deserved." That's when she gave me a powerful hug and I started to laugh and cry at the same time, and then Nanna said I should have something to eat and then go to sleep. I wanted to, but I thought about the men and how 1 had said he would come back for me. I took a piece of rope and tied the angry man's pistol around my waist — I wanted to have a gun close to me every second. Next, I moved our camp a mile or so away, into a deep gully that would hide General O'Brien and the light from our fire from anyone on the trail. So now I am sitting almost on top of our tiny fire, the pistol in my lap, writing this and hoping the night will pass quickly. Mr. Anderson had once said we were "pioneers in a great American adventure," but I am not sure he meant an adventure that included fever and drownings and bandits. End. TAV

Friday: We had walked only a little way when we saw the first wagon coming toward us from Rapid City. It wasn't Poppa or anyone from the Opportunity train, but a group of men coming from the silver fields. "It's a bust," 1 of them told me after I asked if they had seen our people. "Not 'nough silver ta fill a tooth. Yer daddy'll be headin' home soon 'nough, Missy." Nanna and I decided to stay where we were and wait to see if the men came back up the trail. I was so tired, I fell asleep, but Nanna stayed awake and said that all morning men — some in little groups, some by themselves — wandered by, every one of them looking used up and disgusted. I woke up and pretty soon along came Mr. La Brie's wagon with some of the men from the train — but not

Poppa or Uncle Eugenio or the others from our street. These men told us that the *Black Hills Pioneer* had reported the strike as soon as it heard about it so it would be the first with the news and never bothered to really verify it. When the chief assayer got around to examining the claim, he found only copper and some other minerals, but nothing exciting and certainly nothing worth leaving a family behind for. The men thought our people would be along any time now. They were very upset when I told them about the sickness in the train and read out the names of the dead and sick from my diary. They left us some food and water, then hurried up the trail. It might have been an hour or 2 before I spotted Poppa, who hugged me and kissed me, all the time asking why we were there and what was the matter and why was I so dirty and why did I have a pistol tied around my waist and a big bruise on my chin. Nanna answered for me, "While you are off with your silver, your families are sick with fever. Stop talking and get on your horses!"

That's what they did. I got up behind Poppa, and Uncle Eugenio held General O'Brien's lead while Nanna rode him. Then both Nanna and I took turns telling them what had happened since they left — with Nanna saying they were foolish men every so often. None of them argued with her about it. End for now. TAV

Later: Went along all day without stopping. We did halt for a few minutes at the spot where the 2 men had tried to take General O'Brien and our supplies, while Nanna and I went over that story 1 more time. Late in the afternoon, Poppa, Uncle Eugenio, Nanna, and I left the trail and headed straight for our wagons — as straight as I could direct them, that is. The other men continued north up the trail toward the rest of the train and their families. Poppa was for not stopping at all, but all the animals were snorting and exhausted, and I told Poppa that there was a day's ride still and uphill at that. Poppa did not want to hear me and I did not want to argue, especially not in front of Nanna and Uncle Eugenio, but I knew I had to do something. We might hurt the animals if we went any farther and then where would we be? So I hopped off Poppa's horse and stopped General O'Brien to help Nanna off, and said, "This is a good spot to stop." Nanna must have understood, because she got off and said, "Listen to the girl. She was smart enough to scare away bandits and find you, so she is smart enough to know where to camp." Poppa might have argued with me, but not Nanna, so we made camp.

Nanna began preparing supper, while Uncle Eugenio started a fire. That's when Poppa told me how they had traveled down past a town called Belle Fourche when they heard the silver strike was all a story. The town was nothing but confusion — men arriving from every direction, stores and saloons overflowing, the sidewalks and streets jammed, and everyone talking and arguing about the same thing. Some of the men decided to continue, just in case this recent news was just a rumor meant to discourage would-be miners. Uncle Eugenio wanted to go on too, but Poppa said no and turned around, and the others followed. Poppa said he and Eugenio had a very big fight, but that he had missed us so much and worried about us so much that he knew he'd made a mistake in hunting for silver. "I could have told you that before you left," I said, and immediately felt ashamed and sorry that I had said it out-loud, but Poppa didn't seem to mind. "And your Momma did tell me. But I was too stubborn to listen then and . . . well . . ." He didn't want to say it but I knew it was something about Uncle Eugenio and how he always seemed to be led around by him. And I think he knew that I knew because he said, "But it won't happen in the future, Teresa. Not ever again. This is a land where everyone can start over fresh. Even me." I hugged Poppa and he hugged me, and then Nanna said it was time for supper. To bed. End. TAV

Saturday: Poppa said we are leaving as soon as he has General O'Brien packed. Uncle Eugenio wants to have something to eat, but Poppa said we will eat while riding. So we are *all* leaving. Now! Just before we set out, Poppa picked up the pistol and was looking at it when Uncle Eugenio said that he had always wanted a pistol and would like to have it. Poppa did not say anything at first, but instead handed the pistol back to me. "Teresa is the 1 who came by it, so it is hers to give or not, not mine." Uncle Eugenio asked me for the pistol, and when I hesitated, he said, "What use is a pistol to a girl?" "The same as for a boy," I answered, and tied the string around my waist and said I wanted to keep it. I wanted Uncle Eugenio to know that out here we are all starting over again.

Later: We traveled for several hours this morning before stopping. I think we are going in the right direction, but nothing looks familiar to me. Poppa is impatient to go — and so am I — but I told him the animals need more rest or they could get sick. "You are probably right," Poppa said, but he is so anxious that he is off now pacing in the dust and grass and kicking at stones. Uncle Eugenio told him he should relax and that everything would be all right, but Poppa just keeps going back and forth, back and forth.

Still later: Another stop. The horses and mule are thirsty and tired, and Poppa is annoyed and wants to get going. Mr. Bulleau would smile to see him, I'm sure. Uncle Eugenio told him everyone is fine, come, sit and relax and have some bread, but Poppa pulled away from him and asked, "How do you know how Marta and Rosaria are? Or Ernesto? Or the others? How do you know?" "We have to rest the animals," Uncle Eugenio tried. "Kicking up dust won't help them." Poppa walked away, and Uncle Eugenio came back to us shaking his head. "There is no reasoning with him these past days," he said. I wanted to say, "This is only the start," but I stopped myself. It is true, of course, but saying so will not help anyone now.

Another stop to water animals: Came on a stream — which I do not remember at all. But the land is beginning to tilt up more steeply and that feels familiar. Poppa hasn't said very much at all since our last stop and I am worrying too. Everyone is very quiet.

Night-time: We have stopped to eat, but Poppa says we are going to continue in the dark. He said we will have a better chance of seeing their fire and I hope that is true. Just before the sun disappeared, I turned around and thought the Black Hills and other cliffs and buttes looked like they were all in the same position as when we left, so maybe we are near the wagons. Uncle Eugenio did not argue with Poppa, and Nanna is hurrying so we can be on our way. I am going to say a prayer that Poppa is right.

Sunday the 1st

Tuesday: I tried to write on Sunday, but could not. And did not try on Monday. I'm not even sure I can write today, but will try before I forget the details. I can't explain why but I do not want to forget the details.

We continued in the dark on Saturday night, tho slowly, stopping often to search for signs of a fire. Then we saw a thin trail of smoke and sparks floating up into the sky. It was far away, so it took a while to get near enough to actually see the fire. Even then, we weren't sure we had found our wagons, the night was so black and it was hard to see clearly. But as we got closer, we could see the shape of 2 wagons, and then I saw Zephaniah and Red Top grazing nearby.

We tried to get General O'Brien to speed up, but he wouldn't, so we called out to let everyone know we were coming. When we were very close Momma came out of the tent and peered into the dark toward us. "Is that you?" she asked. I could see her cross herself. "Oh dear God, thank You, thank You." It was not like Momma to say such things out-loud, and it made me shudder.

Momma hurried out to meet us, rushing first to embrace Poppa and say how thankful she was to see him and all of us. Uncle Eugenio asked about Aunt Marta and Rosaria, and Momma said they were both fine, tho tired, and Uncle Eugenio went to check on them. "And Ernesto?" Poppa wanted to know. "He is safe," Momma said, and then her hands went to her face and she began to cry. "But our sweet Antoinetta . . ."

She didn't say it. She didn't have to. It was clear from the way she was shaking what had happened. I felt a numb, tingly feeling traveling from my head down my back and arms and suddenly I was so tired, my legs felt heavy and useless. Momma said, "I tried everything I knew . . . everything. . . ." "No, no," Poppa said softly, "I know you did what you could. We know." Nanna did her best to comfort Momma too and said, "She is in heaven now, smiling down on us." I stood on the side feeling empty and cold and hoping someone would hug me too. "You must pray for your sister," Nanna told me, but then she saw my tears and she came over and put her arms around me, and then Momma and Poppa did the same, and Nanna said to us all, "She was so sweet, so sweet. It is more than a heart should ever have to bear."

Netta had died on Friday, in the afternoon, just about the time we left the main trail from Rapid City and headed toward the wagons. The fever came over her on Thursday and got worse quickly. Momma did not want to tell me many details, but from the little she did say it must have been horrible for poor Netta. The next morning, her breathing was labored and then it stopped completely. Momma said she refused to believe Netta was gone at first and hoped that she was only sleeping. But she really knew the truth. When she was sure, really sure, she went and dug a little hole outside of camp. Next, Momma washed Netta and dressed her in a clean dress, then wrapped her in a piece of canvas and put her in the grave. Momma apologized over and over as she was telling us this, sorry that she could not give her little girl a better burial, and I couldn't help crying, I felt so bad for Momma and Netta, wishing I could have been there to be of some help.

Poppa was very quiet when Momma told us all of this, his eyes so sad and lost-looking. He said it was his fault for not being there, for taking us out of New York, for . . . but Momma did not want him to say this and Nanna told him to hush, as if he were a little boy. "Only

God knows why He let this happen," Nanna said. After a while, Poppa said he would make Netta a good coffin to keep her safe, and Uncle Eugenio, who is so quiet you would think it was Rosario who had died, said he would help.

Later Momma said to me, "I found these in her pocket, Teresa. Pages from your diary." She handed me the tissuey, yellow sheets, each covered with Netta's neat hand-writing. No matter where Netta went or how she felt, she had neat hand-writing. If she has to write in heaven, I'll bet hers is the neatest hand-writing of all — neater even than St. Peter's and he has to write in the great book as everyone enters heaven. I am going to paste in her pages now.

Wednesday, June 27, 1883

Dear Aria,

Teresa and Nanna rode off early this morning. I wanted to tell them they were a sight with Nanna perched up high on General O'Brien's back surrounded by all sorts of things for the trip, and Teresa wearing such a long, sad face inside her bonnet. But I did not want to send Teresa off angry at me, so I'll wait for her return to tell her. Maybe she will cheer up when she finds Poppa. After they left, I stood on the wagon seat and waved to them for a long time. Once I yelled to Teresa, but

I do not think she heard me. Aunt Marta did, though, and thought it was Indians coming for us, so Momma said to stop yelling. I am going for a walk alone.
Sincerely, Antoinetta

Wednesday, June 27, 1883

Dear Aria,

My stomach hurts again. When we were on the train my stomach also hurt, but it went away in a few days and I guess this will too. The Shaker Almanac doesn't say anything about fevers, but I did find a letter in it from Malinda Ford of Grand Detour, Illinois, who said the Shaker Extract had cured her son's cough when nothing else had. Her letter was nice, but I liked what was written underneath better: "What ship carries more passengers than the Great Eastern? Courtship." I will show that to Teresa when she gets back and ask her if her ship will be named the John Wilson!
Sincerely, Antoinetta

Thursday, June 28, 1883

Dear Aria,

Our patients all seem a little better. I wish I could say that my stomach was better, but it is not. Neither are my head nor eyes. Even my fingertips ache! I do not want to tell Momma, so I am going to sit under the wagon and rest. I will talk more later.

Sincerely, Antoinetta

Thursday, June 28, 1883

Dear Aria,

Very hot and so am I. Every little noise hurts. I am going to rest more now.

Sincerly, Antoinetta

When I saw that Netta had misspelled Sincerely, I felt myself smile because I had found a mistake of hers at last. Then I remembered and was sad all over again. End. TAV

Tuesday still: We reburied Netta in the afternoon, and I think Momma is glad that has been done. Poppa used sideboards from the wagon to make a solid box, then sealed the cracks inside and out with axle grease. He left Netta wrapped in the canvas — he said it would keep her warm and dry — nailed and sealed the lid in place, then put the coffin in the hole, which Uncle Eugenio had dug deeper. We all gathered stones and piled them on top of the dirt until we had a large enough pile to keep out animals. Even Ernesto managed to leave the tent and put a small stone on. Then we all recited prayers, tho I just said the words and did not really pray. I was thinking of how Netta would never write in my diary again and how I would miss her following me around and writing about it. End. TAV

Later: Very quiet night. Some coyotes are about, but they are not talking much. Everyone is very tired, but Ernesto asked for something to eat. When I brought some bread in to him, I noticed his eyes were red and blotchy and he was sniffing a lot. "It should have been me, not Netta," he said. I was going to say he was just being silly, but I could see he was trying to be brave, so I said, "Netta knows how you feel, Ernesto. We all do." End. TAV

Wednesday: Uncle Eugenio wondered if we should think about catching up with the train before it leaves us completely behind. Poppa said there was no rush and that we would stay a few days so Ernesto and Momma and I could rest, but I think it is something else too. Neither Momma nor Poppa wants to leave Netta, not yet anyway, and neither do I. I want to stay to make sure she is all right. If Netta were here she would write that we are all being silly, because a dead person can never be all right again no matter how long we stay, and I know that's true. But I want to stay anyway. For a while. But the talk of the train did get me thinking about the people there, especially Mary Margaret and J.W. Momma and Poppa and Nanna are here, of course, but I would like to have someone else besides them to talk to about Netta and how I feel. End. TAV

Thursday: Today around noon, we saw a rider heading toward us from the direction of the train. He was far away, 2 or more miles, I would guess, so we could not tell who he was, but we could see that he was leading a packhorse with supplies. I was hoping it might be J.W. coming to take me away from this terrible dream I was stuck in and I could almost see him sitting very tall on his horse and smiling a special smile just for me. So I almost laughed out-loud — and Netta would have too! — when the rider finally came near and I saw it was Shep. I wasn't upset, tho. I think these past weeks and days have taught me that out here what you hope for is 1 thing and what happens is something else completely.

Shep told us that he'd gotten back from the silver mines, heard about us, and set out right away to bring us fresh water and food. He said he was sorry that he hadn't gotten here in time to be some help to Netta, and Momma said he was "a kind soul for saying that." Shep looked embarrassed and said, "Don't know much 'bout that, Mrs. Vees-car-dee. Alls I know is I told Mr. Keil back in Watertun that I'd watch over ya an' I allwas keep ma word no matter what." But he looked pleased about Momma's words, and Nanna went out of her way to cook him a fine lunch. Shep also brought us news. The fever kept striking down people even after the train reached the water. Mr. Anderson was sick, but has recovered, and the same happened to Mr. Keil. But others weren't so lucky, and Shep says that when he got there he found 8 new graves, and many sick. A number of families — Shep guessed 5 or 6 — abandoned the train and the idea of going to Opportunity altogether and went off on their own. But Mr. Bulleau was still there and still willing to lead the train across Montana, thru the Lemhi Pass, and into the Idaho Territory. According to Shep, Mr. Bulleau said he'd been paid to bring us there and he would even if it was just 1 wagon and took a year to do it! "That man's mighty stubern," Shep said, "but it heps ta be stubern out here." Then Shep handed me a tiny envelope with a note from Mary Margaret.

Dear Teresa,

I don't have time to write a long letter, so these few words will have to do. My mother is ill, but not badly, and my father, sister, and I are fine. I hope your brother has recovered and that you are not sick with the fever. Who will I talk to if you get sick? Shep will tell you all that has happened here, but I wanted to tell you that I am waiting for you and that you should get everyone healthy and hurry up because I miss talking to you.

Your Friend, M.M.

P.S. A certain young gentleman has been wandering around camp looking very lost and alone. I said hello to him yesterday and he asked, "Have you heard from Teresa?" I believe that this young gentleman misses a certain young lady a great deal.

Friday: Shep left this morning to see if there were any other families still behind us who might need help. He told Mr. Keil he would do this and then report back on how many of the trailing wagons would be going to Opportunity besides those in the main camp. Poppa said that when he comes back this way we should be ready to go with him, and I have to say there was a part of me that was happy to hear this. Nanna said, "Good. When the dead are buried, it is time for the living to move on." Still, I worry that when we are out of sight of Netta's grave I will forget her, just as I have forgotten Francesca's voice and so many other things from our street. End. TAV

Saturday the 7th

Aunt Marta and my cousin are feeling much better, and so is Ernesto. Whenever I thought about Netta, I expected her to appear and say it was all a joke. But then I would remind myself that she will never be back, ever, and I'd feel tired and empty. Of course, Nanna kept me busy with chores so I did not have a chance to sit and feel sad for too long. "If your hands are moving," she said, "then your head will not fill up with so many thoughts." Poppa and Uncle Eugenio spent the day repairing the wagons and getting them ready to travel. Momma cleaned the wagons and took care of the sick and said everyone would be well enough to travel in a day or 2. End. TAV

Sunday the 8th

Spent the day packing the wagons so there would be room for the sick and a helper, which means we will have to leave many things behind. I also loaded up the canvas sling with bits of wood and bone for our fire. I would not say things are back to normal yet — everyone is still very quiet for one thing — but the day felt more comfortable and I did not have so many thoughts about Netta. Poppa said our hurts would heal in time, but that we would never forget Netta or what she was like. When he said that, I had an idea and decided I needed to visit Netta by myself. I told Momma and at first she looked worried and said it was very dark out where her grave was. Then she reconsidered and said I could go, but that I should take along my pistol in case of snakes or coyotes, which I will do. More later.

Later: I left camp and went to Netta's grave, which is up the hill 100 paces and has a wide-open view of everything around it. Once away from the wagons, it became very dark, almost black, and I have to admit I was nervous enough to take hold of the pistol for comfort. But I found the grave and sat down next it, then reached out 1 hand to touch a cold stone.

I waited a minute while the stone warmed, listening to the sounds of insects buzzing and sun-dried grass rustling and coyotes talking. "Netta," I said out-loud, and my voice cracked a little. I wanted to say her name, to see how it felt in my mouth, to know it was all right to say it. Then I told Netta that I missed her and the way she was always reading my private thoughts and making comments about them, and how she was always correcting my spelling and all of the other things she did. If Netta could have, I bet she would have said I was crazy to be talking to a dead person, but I don't care. It felt good to say these things out-loud. Then I told her what Poppa had said about the hurt going away and what I planned to do — that from now on I will call my diary Netta. In this way, I can talk with Netta my diary directly, and maybe I will not miss Netta my best friend and sister so much.

I looked around then. Below me, the camp-fire gave off just enough light to let me see the shapes of our wagons and tents and animals. And I could see my parents, Uncle Eugenio, and Nanna moving around the fire, talking quietly and getting ready to go to sleep. Not much else was visible — not the distant Black Hills, or the rolling hills of grass, or the light from another fire. A cool breeze was blowing — the wind never stops out here — and I suddenly wished that the Indians were there to sing and drum for Netta. Then I saw it, out of the corner of my eye, a streak of twinkling bright light, a shooting star maybe, moving across the sky. There 1 second, then gone into the blackness of the universe the next. That was Netta in heaven, I told myself, where she will drive Saint Peter and all of the other saints and angels crazy with her little sister know-it-all antics for all eternity, which made me smile and cry at the same time. I said good-night to Netta then, and went back to camp. End for now. TAV

Dear Netta,

I have been waiting to write something happy for you to hear. On Wednesday, Shep came back for us, along with 3 other wagons, and we set out immediately — after saying good-bye to you — to find the rest of the train. Poppa drove 1 of the other wagons because the man had died and his wife was still sick, so I drove our wagon. It was slow going and every time I asked Shep how far we had gone or how far we had to go, he would say, "Every step is a step closer," which I think is Shep's way of saying he doesn't know.

Thursday and Friday we traveled along like this, not hurrying and stopping often. Once when Uncle Eugenio worried about the rest of the train leaving us behind, Poppa said, "Idaho is not ever going to move, Eugenio. We will find it." Ernesto and Rosaria felt stronger and each took turns riding next to me and asking me questions about driving.

But that is not what I wanted to write about. On Saturday, around noon, I was leading our small group when we came over a great grassy bump of land and saw the train of wagons down below near a pond. There were fewer wagons than I remembered, due to those who had pulled out, but there they were anyway, with women,

men, and children moving from wagon to wagon, making repairs, cooking, talking, caring for animals, playing.

We plunged down the hill, and as we did, Shep rode forward and let out a whoop and waved his hat to those below. Everything seemed to stop a moment down there, as people looked to see who was calling. And then people began coming toward us — it seemed like all of them, tho that could not be — some running, some walking. I could hear distant shouts of hello and how are you and then I spotted J.W., who jumped on his horse, spurred it, and came flying up to greet us. Mary Margaret was there too, and her mother, and Mr. and Mrs. Hesse, and Mr. Anderson and — well, you can picture it. A sea of familiar smiling faces.

Mr. Keil emerged from the crowd. He had changed from his black clothes into those of a cowboy, complete with a big, wide-brimmed hat, and looked even sillier than before if that's possible. But his voice was strong and booming and reassuring, like the first time we heard him speak. When I saw them all, I felt myself smiling wide. "We were worried about you," Mr. Keil called to our little group. "Welcome home."

I will always miss my friend Francesca, and my teacher Mrs. Curran, and Nicola, and everybody from our street. That will never change. But do you know what, Netta? I think Mr. Keil is right — about this being home. We are together, Momma, Poppa, Nanna, Ernesto, Tomas, and me, and we have our thoughts about you and everybody else, and we are surrounded by all of these people who care about us. And in a few days, Mr. Keil told us, we will all leave for the Idaho Territory and Opportunity, and I can't wait to tell you all about it. I will talk with you again soon.

Your forever sister, Teresa Angelino Viscardi

Epilogue

Teresa and her family, and everyone else on the train, completed the grueling trip to Idaho and established the town of Opportunity in a broad valley that was even more beautiful than Mr. Keil had described. True to his word, Mr. Keil had roads put in, built a sturdy school and meetinghouse, and organized groups for the construction of houses and the clearing of land.

Both Viscardi families did well in Opportunity. Uncle Eugenio and Aunt Marta lived above their dry-goods store for nearly four decades and were the first in town to have running water, an indoor bathroom, electricity, a telephone, a radio, and a car. Rosaria married when she was seventeen and moved to Arizona, where she had four children and carried on a lively correspondence with Teresa.

Meanwhile, the earth bloomed under the loving attention of Teresa's father, who experimented with many different crops and eventually bought up three additional plots on which he planted apple and peach trees. Her mother took in occasional boarders to supplement the family income and taught nearly one hundred children how to play the piano during her lifetime. Ernesto went off to college in California and studied to be a horticulturist; Baby Tomas never left Opportunity and eventually took over the running of the family farm when his father retired; Nanna, who lived to be ninety-six, dispensed words of wisdom — in Italian and English — to family, friends, and anybody else she encountered.

Just one year after the founding of Opportunity, Teresa was asked to help teach school by Mr. Cross, the head teacher. "Your sister said you were the smartest person she ever had met," Mr. Cross told her, "aside from herself, of course." Teresa assisted Mr. Cross for six years, then took over as head teacher when he retired, a position she maintained until her retirement in 1936.

Teresa never did marry J.W., despite Edi's prediction. He asked her to marry him four times before she was nineteen, but she always said no. She never told him why she would not marry him, but she did tell Netta. "J.W. is a good man and a dear, kind friend, and he will do great things in his life, but you were right. He does not laugh enough, and a life without laughter is a life without surprises, and that is something I could not bear."

When Teresa was thirty-six she met and married James Madden, a member of an itinerant harvesting crew that worked the region at the turn of the century. They had three children, all of whom went to college, and they lived a very simple, spare life. Just one week before her death, Teresa was able to write in her diary:

July 9, 1952

Dear Netta,

The children, and their children, and *their* children have all left, so now the house is quiet at last and I have time to write again. I wanted to tell you about little Jackie, Barb's girl, the one who reminds me a lot of you. She came up to me the other day and demanded, "Where is your television, Nanna? We have one, you know, and Daddy said if it doesn't explode we'll get another soon." I tapped the side of my head and said, "I have all the pictures I need up here." "Really!" she said. "Can I see them if I look in your ear?" I laughed so loud that Jackie began laughing and so did others around us. I realized then that, despite some sad moments and some hard times, I have had one of the happiest lives of anybody I know. It might not be much, but I don't know many people who can say that and really mean it, do you? I can hear James banging around in the kitchen, which means he is looking for something and can't find it. You would think he would know by now to wear his glasses! I will close and talk with you later. End for now. Your sister, TAV

Life in America

in 1883

Historical Note

꘎

From the arrival of the first European colonists in the early seventeenth century, America has been a land of religious, social, and economic experimentation. The Pilgrims fled religious persecution in England and economic insecurity in Holland to establish a colony at Plymouth, Massachusetts, during the winter of 1620. Even before stepping ashore, the travelers asserted the uniqueness of their experimental settlement when forty-one adult males signed the Mayflower Compact, a document that, among other things, declared annual elections for a governor and his assistants. No longer would the Pilgrims be ruled by a nonelected king or his hostile church!

Under the careful guidance of their second elected governor, William Bradford, the Plymouth Colony prospered and grew powerful. Unfortunately, the idea of religious freedom did not extend to anyone outside of their church, nor did it even allow a member to openly question the government or the religion. One member, Roger Williams, was hounded out of Massachusetts for his outspoken criticism and, along with the support of others, such as Anne Hutchinson, founded Providence, Rhode Island. Here another experimental colony — and the first truly democratic one — was set up, where the functions of the church and government were separated, where all religions were welcome, and where freedom of expression became an operating principle and not just words on a paper.

And so it has gone throughout the past three hundred years. One small group of individuals after another would detach themselves from a larger, more established community to create another that promised religious, economic, or social reform — and sometimes all three. Some of these groups are fairly well known to us, such as the Shakers or the Amana colonies, while others, such as the Harmonial Vegetarian Society, the Association of Brotherly Co-operators, and the German Colonization Company, came and went pretty quickly. So far, over 140 such utopian societies have been identified, with the largest number being founded between 1870 and 1900.

These communities seem to have had three things in common. First, they were generally established far from urban centers. Of course, land was cheaper the farther one got from the big cities, but a more practical reason was that such distance allowed these societies to operate without interference. Second, these communities usually relied on and required some sort of communal labor and sacrifice. And third, most were headed by energetic and charismatic leaders who wanted to see their ideas and ideals become a living reality.

Some of these leaders were cruel, egotistical individuals who exploited the zeal of their followers for their own benefit. But many were good, honest men and women who guided their followers with compassion and fairness and shared in the hardships and work imposed on the group.

The real William Keil, on whom the character of the same name in this book is loosely based, seems to have been a blend of both. Many of his followers considered him abrasive and autocratic, but many more saw him as a positive force in their lives. Whatever the truth, he was able to establish two communities, one in Missouri (1844), and the other in Oregon (1854), that managed to survive and prosper as cooperative enterprises until 1881. And he really did bring his dead son Willie west in a lead-lined, alcohol-filled coffin.

America in 1883 was a land caught between two eras. The Industrial Revolution had taken firm hold and allowed millions of people to leave their farms to seek work in factories. Modern conveniences, such as the electric light and telephone, had been developed and were being used in increasing numbers. And a massive railroad system made travel east of the Mississippi quick and easy, while a transcontinental route ran through the center of the United States to California.

But America was still very old-fashioned in many ways. Most people had to live and work on farms, using horse-drawn plows, wagons, and equipment. There was still what many people referred to as the "Indian problem" out West (though most Native American tribes had already been forced onto reservations by this time). And while railroad companies were building lines west of the Mississippi in hopes of connecting all states in a spiderweb of steel rails, most of these would not be operating until the end of 1883 or later. A journey to the West meant using modern steam power for as far as possible, then relying on horse, mule, or ox muscle for the remainder of the trip. This could be a short hop of fifty miles, if one were lucky, or several hundred, depending on how wild and desolate the region happened to be.

Such a journey was always a physical and emotional trial, sometimes even greater than leaving behind friends and family or living in an experimental community with strangers. This was especially true for girls.

They usually left their homes proper young women — clothes neat and decent, hair brushed, nails clean. But the close confines of a hot, steamy train, the frequent bouts of food poisoning, and the rigors of wagon travel soon brought about a transformation. Dust covered their clothes and shoes, nails were broken, skirts were singed by the open fires, hair went unbrushed for days on end. This happened even as horrified mothers (and sometimes grandmothers) urged and ordered these girls to remember there was an unwritten code of conduct they should follow. It happened because traveling through wild territory was always hard and sometimes dangerous, and everyone — girls, mothers, and grandmothers — had more important things to think about and do.

There were positive consequences to this type of travel, of course. Girls were often required to solve problems usually left to the men and boys. They did work they had never done before — such as drive a fully loaded wagon over rough terrain; they faced sickness and death, sometimes on a daily basis; they often lived and functioned on their own with little or no help. These things left girls with a stronger sense of self — they could do the work, they could overcome obstacles and fear, they could survive.

An experimental community held out the hope of freedom and emotional security. Girls often found these qualities in themselves long before the journey ended.

Before the turn of the century, thousands of Italian families had emigrated from various parts of Italy, including the island of Sicily. Italian women and girls mostly wore plain dresses. Boys and men wore pants, jackets, and fedora hats.

In the bustling marketplace in what is known today as the "Little Italy" section of New York City, people spoke in their native Italian and could purchase the traditional foods of their homeland such as crusty bread, mozzarella cheese, and prosciutto, a dried, spiced ham. This tight-knit community preserved their rich culture far from home and was a comfort to many immigrants.

The interior of train cars was noisy and crowded with people of many different ethnic backgrounds. Wooden benches provided seating for the passengers but were not comfortable for long periods of travel. Only some trains had the luxury of fold-out bunks pictured here. In the front of each car was a stove for cooking and in the rear a convenience, or bathroom.

Trains traveling west often had to cross narrow bridges high above water such as the Mississippi River. These dangerous bridges were constructed of steel, stone, and wood, and made tremendous noise as trains traveled over them.

Wagon trains moved slowly over rugged terrain. Often, possessions had to be discarded during the journey in order to lighten the wagon and make it easier to maneuver up hills and mountainsides. Wide wheels helped prevent wagons from sinking into the ground or from tipping over.

Although the prairie appeared flat over a great distance, it was actually made up of many small hills and depressions, causing an even greater strain on the animals. Horses were often unable to withstand the long journey, which involved pulling heavy loads across approximately fifteen miles a day. Oxen had greater endurance.

After a long day's journey, women and girls would set up camp, cook, and wash clothes. Clothes and shoes were constantly mended in an attempt to look tidy during the journey. Girls were urged to keep their long dresses clean and to maintain a proper appearance despite the hardships of the journey, although eventually it became clear that this was not practical.

Monotonous days on the endless stretches of flat prairie were sometimes interrupted by a visit to a town where pioneers were able to purchase dry goods, food, and medicine, and could receive and send mail. The town featured here is one of the larger ones the pioneers might have passed through.

"Snap-the-Whip" was a popular game played by children in the nineteenth century. As depicted here in Winslow Homer's drawing, a group of players form a line by holding hands. The player at the front end is the Snapper; at the back end, the Cracker. As the line moves forward rapidly, the Snapper runs back and tries to snap off the Cracker. If the Cracker is snapped off, then he or she becomes the Snapper, and the player next to the end becomes the Cracker. If the Cracker does not fall off then the whip is snapped again.

STRACCIATELLA SOUP

Ingredients:

       1 quart chicken or beef broth

       2 eggs

       1 ½ tablespoons semolina

       2 tablespoons grated Parmesan cheese

In a bowl combine cheese, semolina, eggs, and three tablespoons cool broth and beat for five minutes. Bring rest of broth to a boil and add egg mixture slowly. Simmer for five minutes while constantly stirring. Serves four.

This traditional Italian soup could be easily prepared over an open fire.

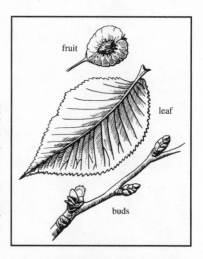

fruit

leaf

buds

Pioneers relied on their natural surroundings for food and medicine. Slippery elm trees reach between 40–60 feet in height and are known for their white, scented, slippery inner bark. Placed in hot water, the bark makes a thick tea known for its many medicinal purposes. It can be applied to burns or fresh wounds to heal the skin.

Many people fell sick and died along the way west. To protect the bodies of the deceased from wild animals, boards from the sides of the wagons were sealed with axle grease and used as coffins. Stones served as grave markers and were inscribed with messages in remembrance of loved ones.

AVE MARIA

Father in Heaven,
gaze on
Thy children,
endlessly!

Father in Heaven!

Father in Heaven!

We call Thee!

Hear us in mercy!

Grant our
souls forgiveness
kneeling before Thee!

Blessed, be Thy name!

O hear our prayer
to Thee,
mercy imploring,

at Thy throne
adoring,

Now and when
we're standing
before Thy throne
of judgment,

Amen!

Amen!

This popular Italian song originated in the 1850s and is still sung today. The beautiful lyrics represent many Italians' devout belief in Catholicism and serve as a comfort, especially while grieving the loss of a loved one.

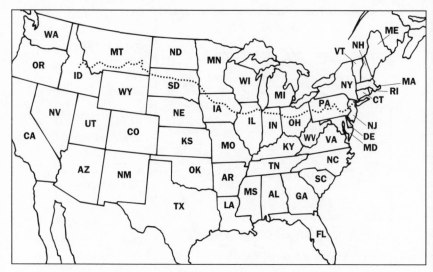

Modern map of the continental United States, showing the route from New York to Idaho.

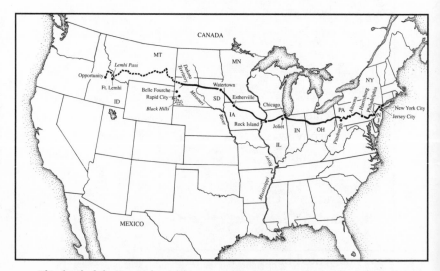

This detail of the New York-to-Idaho route indicates important landmarks and stopping points mentioned in the diary.

About the Author

❦

It's fairly obvious that Jim Murphy's father was Irish. What isn't so well known is that his mother was Italian, whose ancestors came from a village in Sicily. "My mother was outgoing, emotional, and talkative with an unbelievable amount of energy. And when the Italian part of the family got together, the gatherings were always an exciting whirl of noisy conversation, recollections about the 'old days,' family gossip, and well-meaning lectures on how life should be lived, all punctuated with bursts of laughter and an occasional dispute or two. Or three. The characters in both Viscardi families are based to some degree on my mother and her many relatives."

Mr. Murphy was also intrigued by the history of utopian communities in the United States and why people were so eager to join them, especially in the nineteenth century. "These communities offered people various kinds of security, especially to those who felt threatened by the Industrial Revolution or those who were persecuted because of their race or religion. One example is my ancestors from Sicily. They were looked down on as inferior by many other Italians, especially those who lived north of Rome. While none of my mother's people ever joined a utopian society, they did move frequently, seeking job security and neighborhoods where they felt welcome and at home."

Jim Murphy is the author of over twenty-five award-winning books for children. *The Great Fire* was a Newbery Honor Book, as well as the recipient of the NCTE Orbis Pictus Award for Outstanding Nonfiction and a *Boston Globe-Horn Book* Honor Book Award. In addition, *The Boys' War* and *The Long Road to Gettysburg* were both SCBWI Golden Kite Award-winners; *Across America on an Emigrant Train* received an NCTE Orbis Pictus Award; and *A Young Patriot* was given special recognition by the Sons of the Revolution with the Fraunces Tavern Museum Book Award. Mr. Murphy lives in Maplewood, New Jersey, with his family.

Acknowledgments

Grateful acknowledgment is made for permission to reprint the following:

Cover portrait: *The Young Sheperdess* by Adolphe William Bougereau, French, 1825–1905. Oil on canvas, mounted on board, 1885, 62 x 28½ in. (157.5 x 72.4 cm). Gift of Mr. and Mrs. Edwin Larsen, San Diego Museum of Art.

Cover background: *Lightning Express Trains: Leaving the Junction.* Hand colored lithograph by Frances F. Palmer. Currier and Ives. Museum of the City of New York, private collection of Harry T. Peters.

Page 192: Italian immigrants, Library of Congress.
Page 193 (top): Mulberry Street, Corbis-Bettman, New York, New York.
Page 193 (bottom): Interior of train, *Transportation: A Pictorial Archive from Nineteenth-Century Sources,* Dover Publications, Inc., New York, New York.
Page 194: Train on bridge, ibid.

Other Books in the Dear America Series

A Journey to the New World
The Diary of Remember Patience Whipple
by Kathryn Lasky

The Winter of Red Snow
The Revolutionary War Diary of Abigail Jane Stewart
by Kristiana Gregory

When Will This Cruel War Be Over?
The Civil War Diary of Emma Simpson
by Barry Denenberg

A Picture of Freedom
The Diary of Clotee, a Slave Girl
by Patricia C. McKissack

Across the Wide and Lonesome Prairie
The Oregon Trail Diary of Hattie Campbell
by Kristiana Gregory

So Far from Home
The Diary of Mary Driscoll, an Irish Mill Girl
by Barry Denenberg

I Thought My Soul Would Rise and Fly
The Diary of Patsy, a Freed Girl
by Joyce Hansen

Dreams in the Golden Country
The Diary of Zipporah Feldman, a Jewish Immigrant Girl
by Kathryn Lasky

For Michael with love

While the events described and some of the characters in this book may be based
on actual historical events and real people, Teresa Angelino Viscardi is a fictional
character, created by the author, and her diary is a work of fiction.

All rights reserved. Published by Scholastic Inc.
DEAR AMERICA and the DEAR AMERICA logo
are trademarks of Scholastic Inc.
No part of this publication may be reproduced,
or stored in a retrieval system, or transmitted in any form
or by any means, electronic, mechanical, photocopying, recording,
or otherwise, without written permission of the publisher.
For information regarding permissions, write to Scholastic Inc.,
Attention: Permissions Department, 555 Broadway,
New York, New York 10012.

Library of Congress Cataloging-in-Publication Data

Murphy, Jim
West to a land of plenty: the diary of Teresa Angelino Viscardi
New York to Idaho Territory, 1883
by Jim Murphy
p. cm— (Dear America; 8)
Summary: While traveling in 1883 with her Italian-American family (including a
meddlesome little sister) and other immigrant pioneers to a utopian community in
Idaho, fourteen-year-old Teresa keeps a diary of her experiences along the way.
ISBN 0-590-73888-7 (alk. paper)
[1. Frontier and pioneer life — Fiction. 2. Sisters — Fiction.
3. Italian Americans — Fiction. 4. Diaries — Fiction]
I. Title. II. Series.
PZ7.M9535We 1998
[Fic] — dc21   LC#: 97-23064
CIP
AC

10 9 8 7 6 5 4 3 2 1   8 9/9 0/0 01 02 03

The display type was set in Byron.
The text type was set in Dante.
Book design by Elizabeth B. Parisi

Printed in the U.S.A.
First printing, March 1998

∽°∾